CHRISTMAS HOLLY

A Sweet Christmas Volume 5

SAMANTHA JACOBEY

Lavish Publishing LLC

First Edition

A Sweet Christmas Series book 5

2019 Lavish Publishing, LLC

All Rights Reserved

Published in the United States by Lavish Publishing, LLC, Midland, TX

Cover Design by: Victor R. Sosa

Cover Images: CanStock Photo

Paperback Edition

ISBN: 978-1-944985-85-1

www.LavishPublishing.com

Contents

Prologue

GLANCING AROUND HER ANXIOUSLY, Holly tapped the table with the tips of her fingers. She sat in a nice restaurant. Not the best in town, but the napkins were made of cloth. Peeking at her phone, she checked the time. *I got here too early.* She had no idea how the minutes would weigh on her as she sat there.

The woman she waited on was an old friend. *Come on. She was more than that,* her dark side teased. *No, she wasn't,* Holly pushed back. Not really. Their relationship had been complicated, and that made it difficult to put a label on it. Her thoughts slipping into the past, she recalled the few short years they had known each other.

The summer she turned seven, Caroline had moved in directly across the street. A pretty girl, her long blond locks would have been hard to miss, even without the sweet smile. Holly had been a tomboy, so the two of them didn't have much in common those first few days, but they grew on each other. By the end of that first year, they never did anything without the other.

Her thoughts skipping ahead, she recalled the night it all

came to an end. She and Carol had gotten close—too close some would say. Her mother had seen them touching each other in a way they shouldn't have. But they were only fourteen, and both sets of adults had gotten together to discuss the situation, deciding that the girls were young and really didn't know any better.

Sitting at the table, still alone, Holly shuddered. She wanted to drop the memory, the pain of it threatening to drive her away before Carol even arrived. "What good would getting to know her again do anyway?" she mumbled to herself, continuing to look around.

Unable to let go of their history, Holly recalled what happened next—or, what didn't happen. She didn't see Caroline again for nearly two decades, until a scarce three weeks ago. She'd been given a note, written in Carol's elegant hand, before she was put on a plane to go live with an aunt and uncle. She often wondered if it had been coerced. It wasn't hateful, but it was…ordinary—not sounding like the girl she knew so well. Her dear friend had brought color and excitement to her life none since could match.

After that, her life felt empty, with no close friends to speak of. She wasn't left alone with anyone for what seemed like years, as if no one trusted her, especially around other girls. A shrink. A priest. Everyone seemed interested in helping her find the error of her ways. She did her best to be the girl they wanted her to be, but doing so brought no happiness for her. Under her aunt and uncle's watchful gaze, she muddled through high school, feeling suffocated by their constant attention by the end.

Eventually, she'd had enough. When she was barely nineteen, she packed all she owned into two small suitcases, Caroline's note folded and tucked in the side of one of them.

Arriving at a small college, she got a job at a diner and proceeded to pay her own way.

But things never worked out for Holly. Nothing ever felt right in her life—not the jobs, not the school, and certainly not the men. *God, there were plenty of those.* The man of her dreams didn't have to be perfect, but she would have liked to have had decent. *Yeah, I'd have settled for that.*

But the last one cost her three teeth. Her tongue flicked to the side of her jaw, and she unconsciously ran the tip over the bridgework. No one knew the teeth were fake, but she knew. She also knew he would be the last one. *I'd rather be alone than dead.*

A year later, fate took a sinister twist, and on odd happenstance, she ran into Caroline while taking one of her patients for an appointment. It seemed so natural to see her sitting there, with no denying who she was. How they ended up in the same town in itself was beyond belief.

Carol had been so excited to see her. And why wouldn't she be? Holly had been the one forced to move. Holly had been the one treated for her "illness" in an attempt to "fix" her condition. The sweet and innocent Caroline had been left to live her life in peace.

Her nails dug into her palms as she thought about it. *What am I doing here, anyway?* If she had refused to exchange numbers, she wouldn't be, and none of those sad memories would be chipping away at her accomplishments, stealing her success.

"Holly!" A slender blonde slipped into the chair across from her. "I'm so happy to see you!"

That's why. She had never gotten over her. Half her life ago, and she could still taste the one and only time she had kissed her. "Hi, Carol." Her name floated airily from Holly's lips as she stared into her best friend's beautiful blue eyes.

She hadn't forgotten her despite all the pressure and attempts to strip her away. "I only came because you said it was important."

"It is," the other girl assured. "We've had some setbacks at the Ford house, and after seeing you the other day…" She paused, Holly's face appearing almost frightened. "Don't be afraid, love. It's a job. A really good one. Lanelle is going to need a full-time nurse, and, of course, I thought of you!"

ONE

Birthday Girl

"HAPPY BIRTHDAY TO YOU! Happy birthday to you!" Candy sang at the top of her voice.

"Happy birthday, dear Joy," Gary joined in. _"Happy birthday to you._ Make a wish, princess!"

"Oh, Gary! She's too young for wishes." Carol laughed loudly, turning the small cake as she placed it on the tray, a single candle's flame dancing in the center of it. "Blow, Joy!"

Pushing his way to her side and producing puckered lips, Daks demonstrated, helping his sister with the task. "B'ow, Joy'ana!" With a quick puff, the fire flickered and vanished into smoke.

"Yeah!" Candy cheered, using her phone to snap pics while the others posed with cheesy grins. "Oh gosh, that's awesome!" Her daughter grabbed a fistful of the miniature cake and licked it happily off the sides of her hands. "Oh, no." Candy held her grin but cringed at the stains the thick icing made on Joylana's dark flesh. "That'll be fun to clean up."

"Just let her keep licking," Gary advised with a laugh.

"She'll have it gone in no time." Scooping Dakota up, he placed him in a chair. "You're getting too big to lift, son!"

Cackling, Daks imitated his not-so-baby sister as Carol placed a piece of the chocolate dessert before him. Sinking both hands in, he smushed it before using the grimy digits to scoop bites into his mouth.

"Oh, Daks," Candy groaned, still smiling from ear to ear.

From her seat next to her door, Lanelle watched the chaos, her nurse Holly cutting a piece for her and then helping her to connect with her mouth.

"Holly, would you like ice cream with yours?" Carol offered.

The shorter redhead hesitated before accepting the suggestion, recalling that her own family had seemed less accepting of her before she left the home of the aunt and uncle who raised her. She had only been a part of the Ford household for a few weeks, and yet they made her feel like one of the family. "Um, sure."

"Don't be shy." Candy plunked down in the chair across from her, then joined her children, licking at her pink-coated fingers. Her spirits high, she toyed with her mother's nurse.

"I'm not shy," Holly denied, a soft flush painting her cheeks. "Not normally. You're all so energetic it's hard to keep up," she added with a short laugh.

"That's true," Lanelle agreed, her words slightly slurred.

Candy's smile faded, and her eyes grew distant. Noticing the change, Holly focused on her patient. It warmed her heart to see Lanelle enjoying the festive occasion, and her employer's mood swings weren't really any of her business. *I'm not shy, but I know where the boundaries lie,* she mused as she cut another bite of cake for her charge.

"Mumumum," Joylana babbled away with one-year-old glee.

Hearing the chatter snapped her out of her trance, and Candy leaned towards her, producing a smile. "Mumumum," she repeated, certain the sounds were meant for her.

"Mimi," Lanelle countered.

The sweet girl kicked her feet with excitement. "Memememe."

"Dada," he said, his voice pitching up.

"Dadada."

Gary chortled at Joy's compliance.

What a happy day. Holly accepted her share of the dessert, then took turns eating hers and still helping Lanelle when her hand wasn't steady. Lost in her thoughts, she reminisced at the afternoon she had been hired to be Lanelle's full-time caregiver. It wasn't cold yet, but the nip in the air hinted at an early winter and short fall. *The leaves fell almost overnight this year.* Glancing at the back door, she thought about the giant trees in the yard.

Gary and Dakota had been scraping the leaves into large piles when she had pulled into the back drive in her small, brown Honda Civic. Dropping his rake, the tall, handsome fireman had ambled over to greet her and showed her into the house, where Lanelle had occupied her current seat. *Her favorite place to be.*

After introducing everyone, Candy had presented a list of chores that would be specifically hers, all of which were related to the direct care of the girl's mother. They had hired her pretty much on Caroline's say so. *Sweet Caroline.* She blinked rapidly, skipping over the details of their relationship —childhood friends, split when they were teenagers, and only recently reunited by a fluke of chance. *My lucky day,* she thought ruefully, not certain how she felt about it as she settled in her new position.

Inhaling deeply, a soft flush warmed her cheeks as she

thought of her friend. Cutting her eyes over at the blonde, the air escaped in a quiet sigh. As much as she enjoyed being a part of their household, she knew her position there was only temporary, and she felt compelled to keep her focus clear. *I really can't become too involved with these people on a personal level.* She needed to remain professional, as they would all leave her life as quickly as they had come into it, she was certain.

Not exactly in need of a hospice nurse, the family had lured Holly away from just such a facility, and she assumed she would return to work there once her job here was done, however long that might be. She was accustomed to dealing with terminally ill patients. Helping them and their families through those difficult times was a way of life for her. No one was permanent, and she liked it that way. *Simple. Clinical. Painless.*

Smiling as Lanelle played with the birthday girl, she knew this assignment could serve as a break in her routine, as she might have years before Lanelle was ready for the end. *With cases like hers, it's so hard to say what will happen.* "Joy'll be talking before you know it," she chimed in, swept up in the occasion with them.

"Yes, she will." Candy nodded firmly in agreement. "But for now, I need to get back to my studying. My midterms will be here before I know it as well."

"Go on." Carol shooed at her. "We've got this."

"I know you do." Holding her smile, Candice washed her hands in the sink, drying them thoughtfully before sauntering down the hall to the office she and Gary shared. It had been a hard year for them, a hard series of years, but this particular one heralded adjustments that had to be made. First, she had made the huge decision last Christmas to cut back on her schoolwork and had only taken a single class last spring—one designed to improve her writing skills.

She took another over the summer that had solidified her new abilities, and she had dived back in full strength with the fall semester. Things were great for all of four weeks before her mother suffered a series of small episodes, as the doctor had called them. *Mini-strokes.* Not severe, like the major hemorrhage she had suffered a few years ago, but enough to set her back significantly and indefinitely. Lanelle might only live a few months, but she could hang on like this for years, almost trapped in limbo. The not knowing was more difficult than Candy ever could have imagined.

It was then that a choice had to be made. She would either quit school for good and focus on her mother or she would need more help. Carol just couldn't do it all, not with the size of their house and Dakota's special needs. *Holly was our only option.* That was the second change and one that could remain for months or even years. *Until Mom either gets better...or she passes.* She didn't like to dwell on that possible outcome.

Candice sighed as she took her place at the large desk and switched on the computer. She had a few quiz programs she would use to study the material, and they had greatly improved her ability to score well on her exams. *If only life's challenges could be solved so easily.* Her third adjustment was a burden she alone would bear if she could help it.

She and Gary had adopted Joylana a year ago, after another full year of preparing to do so before she came into their lives. Over that time, she had struggled with her methods of birth control, with only partial success. *Oh, it works.* She giggled to herself. The small pills had prevented her from conceiving, but they had brought about unwanted side effects, ones that had forced her to change brands right about the time her mother's condition had plummeted.

Seated at the large desk, she clicked the mouse button, viewing screen after screen. Finishing a round, she leaned back in the leather chair and stretched, her eye drawn to a large picture of Eveline that Gary kept on his desk. The deep brown eyes of her mother-in-law bore into her, as if the woman were there, scrutinizing her as she worked.

Sitting up quickly, Candice snatched up the frame, clapping it down onto the desk, face down. "There." She dusted her hands together loosely. She had promised Eveline, and the rest of the family, she was going to work on her attitude, but it had proven more difficult with all that had happened. Leaning against the flat surface, she hit the spacebar to restart the quiz, her hazel orbs fixed on the screen as she fought for focus.

However, after nearly an hour, she sighed and shut down the machine. Lifting the picture she had struggled to ignore, she scowled. "I know, Eve." Guilt turned her stomach as she realized she had a long way to go to live up to that promise. "I didn't know Mom was going to get so sick so fast," she lamented aloud, still talking to the woman she held in her hands.

Her mood crashing, she sucked her lips in to chew on them, her chin quivering as tears welled in her eyes. Her face bright red, she sniffed loudly, allowing her drops of sadness to spill over and stain her cheeks. "I'll make it up to you," she whispered. "After this thing with Mom is settled. But for now, I really need to keep you out of this."

Eveline Ford had a habit of meddling, a fact that Candy had learned firsthand three years ago when she and Gary had announced their intention to marry. First, the older woman had tried to drive a wedge between them. Little Candice and her ready-made family didn't suit her in the "bride of my son" department. However, after realizing she wouldn't be able to push them apart, Eve had swung the other way and helped Candy deal with the very unpleasant situation created by Dakota's father.

"Nope. You are much too unpredictable, even if you are Gary's mother, and we will be much better off if you leave town as usual and let us handle everything here for ourselves." That decision final, she placed the photo back in its designated location and stood to leave the quiet room, shutting the light off as she went.

TWO

Halloween Tradition

WINEGLASS IN HAND, Eve stood in front of the crackling fire and surveyed the room. The pop and hiss of the embers echoed her mood, and her eyes narrowed as she watched her only son toss back his head and laugh heartily. *What are you up to, Gerald?*

As if he had heard the thought, Gary's eyes flittered over to the tall, slender matriarch of their family. Pursing his lips, he stifled the loud cackle. "Sorry, Rob. I believe my mother would like a word with me."

"No problem." Robert glanced at Eveline as well. "She's been smoldering since they got here. They're leaving for Florida on Saturday?"

"God, I hope so." Gary took a large swig of his chardonnay. "At least I believe they are. Things have been rather unsettled these last few weeks." His eyes misty, he swallowed to hide the ache in his voice. "Enjoy the evening," he added over his shoulder as he worked his way towards her, stepping over children and wedging between chatting adults.

Arriving next to her, he slid his arm easily around her waist for an atypical hug. "Good evening, Mother."

Accepting the gesture, his need to hold her only added to her distrust of the situation. "I notice you've added more help." Her tone almost accusatory, she remained stiff, and he released her after the brief squeeze.

"Observant as always," Gary muttered. Dropping his arm to his side, he squared himself to stand beside her. Before them, their extended family swarmed about the house. Seated in her chair, Lanelle appeared to be the only one not moving. Studying her, he could see her blanket-covered chest rise and fall in rhythm, her closed eyes indicating she was resting them, if not actually sleeping through the chaos of the Ford clan. "Holly isn't really help."

"Oh? Then what is she exactly?"

Cutting his soft brown orbs over while maintaining his position, he could see her intent glare at the kitchen, where Carol and Holly were working to prepare for their evening meal. "She's a nurse, not a housekeeper. She's here to see that Lanelle gets the care she needs."

His mother-in-law's eyes opened at hearing her name. Not moving her head, she flicked them around, locating Gary and Eve to her right and blocking her view of the fire. Swallowing, her lids slowly slid back into place, and she resumed her meditative state.

Wary of her, Gary added quietly, "This really isn't the time to discuss our situation."

"I've decided I'm not going to Florida," Eve countered, leaping off-topic and sending his thoughts scattering.

"You always go to Florida!" His hand trembling, the wine in his glass emitted small waves of shock.

"Not this year." Eve sniffed, punctuating her demand.

"Not this year what?" Roger asked, joining them and claiming his wife's left side. Turning his back on Lanelle, he hoped to keep the conversation between the three of them despite the number of people bustling around the room.

"I wish to remain in New York," Eve insisted. "I know something is going on here, and I wouldn't feel right being so far away should anything happen."

Meeting his father's gaze, Gary drank from his glass. Lowering the crystal goblet, he soothed, "Nothing is going to happen, Mother. Besides, I think what everyone needs right now is normalcy. We need the calm that comes from routine, and you staying wouldn't help."

"Because I'm not wanted?" Something was definitely going on—something she had not been made privy to.

"It isn't that, love." Roger hid what he knew behind an even tone. "You and Candy get along, but you have never been close. This business with her mother is her concern, and you should stay out of it." His voice snapped at the end, imploring her not to make a scene.

"So, you admit there *is* cause for concern," she accused.

"I admit my wife is a stubborn old woman who can't fix everything no matter how badly she would like to," he tossed back, forcing a smile. "Please, Eveline."

"And what am I supposed to do? Go putter around on a golf course and check in with the occasional conference call as if everything were normal?" Tears formed in her eyes, and she blinked rapidly to hide them. True, she and Candy had never been close, but that didn't mean she didn't care. To the contrary, she had grown quite fond of the girl and her children. *My grandchildren.* The idea her help was not wanted stung but was nothing compared to the pain of knowing she had been kept in the dark. *On purpose.*

At that moment, Candice came into view as she descended the stairs, carrying Joylana on her hip and holding Dakota's hand as he navigated the steps carefully. All three heads before the fire turned to watch them conquer the final segment, all three hearts filled with love for the girl who had become a part of them and the family that belonged to all of them.

"We all want to be there for her, but she wants to handle this on her own," Roger pointed out in a gravelly tone. "We should honor her wishes."

"She's just a girl." Eve sniffed once more, sipping at her glass and blinking again. "How foolish to think she must always do things on her own."

"Ha." Gary coughed a short laugh. "Reminds me of you, actually. Stubborn. Willful. And deeply caring. Please, Mother. Go to Florida. Putter around the course, and don't let this trouble you too much. Holly is here to help look after Lanelle, and Carol is here for Candy and the kids as always."

"And I would just be in the way," she summarized for him.

"I never said that," he hissed, hoping to end the quarrel before Candy made it to them. "But for now, the discussion is closed." Raising his chin, he smiled broadly, and his voice rose a full octave. "Hello, my princess," he cooed.

Diving towards him, Joy's fingers stretched to claim him as her mother presented a matching grin. "You three seem rather preoccupied this evening."

"We're making our final plans for our departure," Roger stated firmly. Giving Eve a harsh glare, he silently dared her to contradict him. "You know how we love our sunshine."

"Oh, I know." Candy giggled, relief escaping her lips in a small sigh. Her arms freed, she crossed them, rubbing her biceps vigorously as she glanced around at the full house, the lot of them crowded into the warmest parts. There would be no dining on the veranda this year.

Daks had left her to join his cousins, and they were

preparing to leave shortly to make an early pass through the neighborhood in the unseasonably cold evening air. Even Bella had blossomed since the previous year and excitedly shared stories with her cousins while helping them prepare to leave for the annual hunt.

"Come, Joy'ana!" Dakota held up an empty bucket, begging his younger sibling to join them.

Laughing gently at his request, Candy knelt and drew her son to her chest for a firm hug. "Joy can't eat candy yet, baby. Maybe next year we'll take her."

"But want Joy to come."

Marveling at her grandson's improved speech, Eve clasped her hands together in front of her, pressing the palms flat as her fingers curled over the backs. She knew better than to interfere, but the temptation felt overwhelming.

"I know, baby," Candice soothed. "You want me to come? Let me get my coat, and we can go together."

Not satisfied with the replacement, Dakota flung himself onto the floor, the bodies of the adults and older children parting around him as he writhed. "Want Joy!" he shouted.

"On your feet, young man!" Gary's voice boomed. Handing his daughter to Eve, he closed the distance between them and scooped up the boy, placing him over his shoulder and marching towards the kitchen and out the back door into the cool evening air.

Eveline had accepted the infant with a surprised grin. "Why hello, my little angel!"

"I'll take her," Candy offered dejectedly, standing beside her.

"That's quite all right," Eve sang, her mood brightened by the unexpected moment. How much will Joy have changed by the time she returned home in the spring? Gary and Roger both assumed she wanted to remain behind in order to pry in

17

the young family's affairs, but her motives were much simpler and maybe even a little more selfish than that. "I wish I could stay here this Christmas," she blurted, her fingers tracing the sprigs of Joy's dark black hair.

Roger's concerned features snapped to her whimsical grin. "I thought we had settled this."

The tension thick, Candy glanced up at the couple, then towards the back door, where Gary would be working through the process of helping Dakota calm himself. Neither location inviting, she stammered, "I didn't realize your plans weren't firm."

"Oh, they're firm," Roger growled.

"Well," Eve whispered, "you can't fault me for the try." Curling her bundled Joy closer to her chest, she rested her chin atop her head and wished just once their Christmas could be less complicated. "Mind if she sits next to me for dinner?"

"You want to feed her?" Candy gasped, surprise distracting her from the scene out back.

"I've missed caring for a child," Eve confessed. "It's been three decades since Gary needed that kind of care, and I'd love to." She didn't visit with them often, and the regret had settled into her gut like a lump as the colder weather had taken hold. She'd been missing out, but no one seemed to care but her.

"Ok." Glancing at Roger, the girl could see the flush staining his cheeks, and she swallowed. She had never seen him angry, but his genial disposition appeared crushed by whatever they had been discussing before her arrival.

Holding Dakota's hand, Gary led him back into the front room. "I think we're ready," he announced. "Bella, can you help him with the rest of his costume?"

"Sure." Turning to Daks, she added, "Don't worry, little

man. I'm going to make the rounds with you guys, so I'll make sure you get plenty to share with Joy."

Wiping at his tear-streaked cheeks, Dakota nodded. "T'anks, Bell."

Bouncing Joy, Eve's heart fluttered at the grins the action produced. She would never admit her jealousy of Lanelle to anyone, but keeping it hidden did little to remove it. Candy's mother was there for everything, leaving Eve with the scraps of time no one else had claimed. Her decision firm, tonight she wanted more.

Weaving through the adults as the children made their exit, she carried her charge into the dining room, where she realized what that choice would cost her, for the highchair was not to be seen. Lacing her way around, singing as she went, she located the device in its usual location—next to Lanelle's seat at the kitchen table. *Mimi, the favorite grandmother.*

Blinking tears, Eveline struggled to hold the happy moment. She was there, now, holding her granddaughter. *I can't let envy steal my Joy.* Bouncing her a few more times, she considered her options. She could move the baby seat into the dining room, but it had obviously been left in the kitchen on purpose. *If I put her in it where it sits and take Lanelle's chair, I'll catch flack over that.*

As she deliberated, the house grew quiet. Hearing the silence, she glanced around quickly, discovering that Lanelle had entered the kitchen and shuffled slowly towards her sacred place at the old table. The other woman had been tucked in her recliner since she arrived, not moving until it looked like she might lose her seat in the other room, and the guests seemed to pause with bated breath, waiting to see what would happen next. Over her shoulder, Eve could see Carol and Holly stood frozen, observing her reaction to the slow movements of their sickly client.

Turning her attention fully to Lanelle as well, Eve could see that she had missed more than just a few playdates with her grandchildren. Whatever had happened, whatever secret thing they weren't telling her about, it had devastated their Mimi. Her steps deliberate, her feet scarcely left the floor as she moved, her slippers dragging loudly in the stillness as they scooted around the end, behind Joy's highchair. Holly arrived next to her as she reached her goal and helped her to sit on the straight-backed chair. Holding the cushion, her strawberry-red hair glistened as she prevented the cushion from sliding as the older woman sat. The scene unfolding before her, Eve suspected the worst.

Glancing around hurriedly, she blinked wildly at the hot tears that sprang to her eyes. They hadn't told her because there was nothing she could do, exactly as Roger had warned her. Here she had been jealous of…nothing. The weeks and months since Joy had come into their lives had been small compared to the years that lay ahead—years in which Eve would likely play a great part, as at some point, and probably soon, she would be her little angel's only grandmother. No one had told her the end was coming, but watching the other woman settle into her place at their simple table, it troubled her to think that she was right. *This is the secret they are hiding from me.*

Forcing a full fake smile to her lips, one she hoped hid her discombobulated state, Eveline offered, "Here, let's put her between us so we can share."

"Your place is set at the head of the table," Carol informed her, indicating the dining room through the wall with a raised hand. The formal side of their lives had always been Eveline's domain. Why would she trouble herself with what took place in the day-to-day?

"Rubbish. I've sat at the head plenty of times. This year, I want to dine with my beloved Joy and my dear friend Lanelle." Her voice did not shake, and she pulled out the seat across from her to emphasize her intent. "The rest of you go on. Enjoy the feast before the children return."

With the weather so cold and the family so large, it had been a sensible plan to break with tradition. The adults would dine while the children roamed, then the youngsters would eat upon their return. Otherwise, there wouldn't have been enough seats for everyone in their growing brood. Seeing the logic in her proposal, the others reluctantly retired to the dining room, and Gary sat in his mother's place at the head of the table.

Serving their plates and joining them in the kitchen, Carol and Holly exchanged wondering glances and kept the conversation to a minimum, never in their lives expecting to share a meal with the high and mighty Eveline Ford.

THREE

Eve's Advice

SEATED at the aged kitchen table, their granddaughter between them, Eve giggled as she fed Joy bites from her small plate of food. Across from her, Lanelle smiled and cheered along, her words slurred when she spoke, making them difficult to discern. Assisting her with the meal, Holly ate, but Eveline noticed she spent most of the time helping her charge.

"That's my pretty girl." Eve lifted another bite for her, admiring her dark, pudgy cheeks as she chewed the morsel.

"She loves her dinner times," Carol observed brightly.

Holly cocked a crooked grin, waiting for the interrogation she felt certain lay at the heart of the older woman's desire to dine with them. She had only been a part of the household a few weeks, but she had been schooled on the family affairs where she was concerned and would not need reminding that her position there was considered a covert operation, with keeping speculations about the future to a minimum.

However, the questions did not come, and she eventually relaxed in the pleasant company and laughter of the other females. The spectacle seemed to do Lanelle good, as she ate more than she normally did while enjoying Joy's gurgles and babble.

"She'll be talking soon at this rate," Eve observed with a sigh, thinking again of her winter home so far away.

"When do you leave?" Carol asked casually between bites.

"Saturday. Or that's when I should, I suppose. I've voiced my desire to winter here this year, but everyone seems adamant that I should go." Her features drooped, and she took a few bites for herself.

Sharing a glance with her new co-worker, Carol pursed her lips. She knew their guest had not been given details about Holly's presence, and she had no intention of being the one to spill the beans. "Don't you usually enjoy your time in Florida?" The question seemed neutral enough.

"Oh, quite." Eve sniffed loudly. "I have friends in the country club and a few more near the condo. There will be rounds to play and shopping to do. Evenings out at parties and events to attend. It will be great fun, as it is every year." Absently, she raised her hand to caress the pudgy arm of the child next to her.

Watching the motion, it occurred to Holly that she might have been misinformed. That, or the family didn't understand the motivations of Eveline Ford as completely as they thought they did. "You're going to miss Joylana," she observed quietly.

"Very much." Her lip quivered before she sucked it in and held it still. Cutting her doleful eyes over at Carol, she whispered, "Please don't say anything. I wouldn't want to trouble Gary or Candy with my…" Her voice trailed away. Glancing at Lanelle, she didn't make the observation aloud, but she felt certain of what she had seen. "They have other things to worry about."

"Indeed," Holly agreed quietly. Standing, she gathered Lanelle's plate and stacked it with her own, allowing the conversation to drop.

In the crowded dining room, Candy sat to her husband's right, in his previous seat. He occupied the head of the table, which had customarily been occupied by Eveline in years past. Seeing her staring at the wall as if she wished it was made of glass, he leaned closer and whispered loudly, "I don't hear any screams. Perhaps they are getting along."

"Pfft." Candy shuddered, then returned to her meal.

"Son," Roger rebuked with a chuckle. "Your mother is perfectly capable of being civil when the need arises."

"As I am aware. However, she has forgone dinner with the rest of us and is dining in the kitchen with the help. You don't find that a bit odd?" Gary countered.

"She has been behaving a bit strangely," his father confessed. "Perhaps her desire to winter here is more than a desire to intrude."

"No," Candy grunted, noting that the others turned to look at her sharp reply. "I mean, please don't stay on our account. We would be much happier knowing our little setbacks have not interrupted your plans."

"It would be no trouble at all." Seeing her expression unchanged, Roger sighed. Like Eve, he knew there was more to the story, but whatever it was, neither Candy nor Gary would speak of it, and he suspected it had nothing to do with her mother. "Very well. I will see to it that we are on the plane as planned. However, don't be surprised if she puts up a fuss. Eve seems quite adamant this year about staying."

Shaking her head, Paula could see the discontent in

Candice's hazel orbs. When she and Robert had first married, she had felt the same way, but over the years, her dark opinion of their matriarch had softened. As it turned out, she had come to find that Eve's advice was often sound and likely to be as insightful as anyone might receive. However, with Candy, things were different, and in the end, she would have to discover that fact for herself. "I wouldn't judge her too quickly."

"Who, Eve?" Candy hissed.

"Yes, Eve," Matthew snapped, earning a dark glare from Anette. "I'm an outsider, same as you, and I know it can be hard for us coming into a close-knit family such as this," he added smoothly.

"Exactly," Anette seconded. Nodding at her cousin, she grinned. "A year ago, I was horrified to learn we were moving back here, but now that we are settled, I feel like being home has done us a world of good."

Bella leaping into her thoughts, Candice sighed. "I have to agree. You all look much happier. But put yourself in my shoes. Eve and I seldom see things eye to eye, and I would simply rather not deal with it right now."

Silence fell over the table for a long moment, and the subject was dropped as if the conversation had never taken place, much to Candy's relief. Her mother-in-law was her problem and one she was looking forward to ignoring for a good five months while the other woman whiled away the winter several hundred miles south.

Climbing the stairs with Joy drooped on her shoulder, Candy could hear Eve's footsteps creaking the old boards behind her. *Damn.* In years past, the older couple had come for a few hours and then seen themselves off well ahead of the rest of the family. This year, they were the last ones left.

"Well, it was nice you and Roger were able to stay so long," she muttered when they reached the landing, hoping to dismiss her guest and send her back down. "I'll be putting Joy to bed after her bath, so no need to worry you'll be missing anything."

"Oh, I'm not worried." Eve grinned at her. She had spent the evening feeding, holding, and even changing a diaper for her ebony princess. "I've been looking forward to bath time."

"Yes. I'm sure you have." Candy groaned inaudibly, turning and leading the way into the nursery and the adjoining bath that she and Gary shared with Joylana.

"Let me take her," Eveline offered. "You can set the tub, and I'll get her undressed."

"Put on the heater," Candice suggested. "This early frost. It's too chilly to have her wet without the added warmth."

Cutting on the switch, the wires glowed red-hot, and a fan forced the heated air out into the room. Satisfied, Eve placed the infant on the changing table and removed her pretty pink jumpsuit, then wrapped her in a blanket to keep her warm until the water had been drawn. Humming to herself, she thought of a song she had sung to Gary when he was small. "Have you decided on adopting another?"

The question instantly put Candy on edge. Reaching slowly to test the cascade, she held her reply, swallowing a few times to steady her voice. "Perhaps in a few years." Right now, they had other things to deal with—things that put all else on a back burner.

"I think you make wonderful parents. Another child would be lucky to have you." Arriving at the door, Eve leaned on the frame and cuddled Joy as she studied Candy's profile. "Of course, your house may be large, but it's getting quite crowded with so many."

Candy sniffed, and her shoulders jerked. "It's only temporary," she managed.

"I see." Deciding to handle her son's wife with kid gloves, Eve waited. When the pause grew long, she knelt beside her and unwrapped the baby. Testing the water, she carefully placed her in the tub and cut off the flow.

Candy had not moved, her honey-blond hair hiding her face as she fought her sorrow. *Why can't you just go back downstairs?* she silently fumed.

Seizing the basket of toys stashed in the corner, Eve added them to the bath and then sat back on her haunches to watch her granddaughter play for a few minutes before applying the soap. "Candy, I know things are hard right now."

"You don't know anything!"

Taken aback, Eve stammered, "I may not have been told anything, but I'm not stupid, Candice. I know that something has happened with your mother. A nurse. Her physical appearance. I just ate dinner with her, for God's sake."

Candy's head popped up, and she glared at her. Tears streaked her cheeks, a mixture of sorrow and anger roiling inside her. "And?"

"And I'm here if you need me."

The simple gesture stung. Candy had not expected such a thoughtful reply, the heartfelt care reflecting in Eve's typically scornful eyes. It was too much, and she broke into heavy sobs. Glancing at her daughter, she got to her feet and exited via the other door, closing it behind her. Standing in the darkness of her bedroom, the cool air soothed her, and she leaned back against the flat surface.

Eve let her go and located the bottle of lavender-scented gel and the bright pink cloth with which to apply it. Taking care, she cleansed each fold, singing and soothing as she did so while Joy played and giggled, oblivious to her mother's distress in the other room. When the scrubbing was complete, Eve pulled the plug to drain the water and wrapped the wriggling form in a soft, dry towel. "I thought that was supposed to put you to sleep."

"We rock her after," Candy informed her, cracking the door and peeking to see how things were going. Stepping farther in, she turned to the sink and washed her face with cool water, then dried it on the small swath of material that hung on its ring. Joining Eve at the changing table, she produced a fresh onesie and watched as the older, practiced hands applied the clothing. "You haven't forgotten a thing."

"Of course not. These times will be short and will never come again, Candy. Be sure you don't miss a minute of your daughter's babyhood." Eve laughed quietly, certain of Candy's desire to change the subject and instantly regretting what might have sounded like a scolding. "I'll miss so much while we are away. She'll be walking and maybe even talking by the time we return."

Staring at her profile as Eve completed popping the snaps into place, Candy felt a stab of guilt. It was, after all, her insistence that she be removed. "You don't come to visit that often anyway." Holding her nerve, she gathered the jug of water and can of powdered milk to make a bottle. Her fingers shaking while she prepared the formula, she avoided eye contact—avoided the silent struggle that seemed to rage between them.

"No, I'm a busy woman," Eve agreed. "It's better if I go." Her task complete, she stared at the younger woman who would not meet her gaze, noting her son was quite right; his mother and his wife were both stubborn, willful women. "I'll leave you to the rocking." Abandoning the room, she fled down the stairs and located her coat, shoving her arms into the sleeves.

"Are we leaving?" Roger asked in surprise.

"Yes. Now." Eve flung open the door and dove into the chill night air, holding her tears until she had made it to the sanctuary of their car so no one would know how hard she had cried.

FOUR

The Good Stuff

ALLOWING HER MOTHER-IN-LAW TO FLEE, Candy curled Joylana into her arms and rested back into their rocking chair. Staring at the bottle she had been making before Eve abandoned them, she contemplated that it would be one of their last. When their current supply ran out, they would be transitioning to milk, and a few weeks after that, they would lose the bottle and go with cups only.

"I didn't realize how fast you would grow." She sighed as she placed the nipple within reach, and Joy eagerly pulled it in to suckle. Her large round eyes a deep ebony, they stared up at her, and her tiny fingers splayed to help hold the bottle in place.

Out in the hall, commotion echoed as Gary and Daks came up the stairs. "Shh. Mommy is putting Joy down."

Daks giggled a crazy laugh but obediently darted into his bedroom and then his bathroom, the one that joined his room with Carol's. Also making the turn, Gerald placed the plug in the tub and started the water while Dakota stripped down and prepared for his bath.

"Did you have a good time tonight?" Gary's voice faintly trailed into the room across the hall, giving Candy a smile.

"Had fun," Daks assured.

Noticing Joy had begun to doze, Candy continued her gentle rocking, the chair creaking faintly as the noises of the bath soon drowned out any further conversation. Her thoughts roaming, she considered Eveline's odd behavior. Everyone had agreed at dinner that she had not been herself as of late.

Pushing the issue aside, her thoughts turned to Lanelle. Air escaped her lips loudly once more, as thinking of her mother had become far more dismal. Candy had taken time off to balance her life, but as Christmas approached, she felt as unbalanced as ever. She loved her daughter and son, but she needed to do some things for herself.

And then there's Mom, Eve, Gary... Candy's thoughts ran in circles. "I've made all these plans and commitments, never realizing how each would affect the other." It seemed like the universe was conspiring against her, and the emotional turmoil her birth control brought on...

Shifting Joy to her shoulder and dropping the empty bottle to the floor, Candy continued to rock her. Not ready to put her down in the bed, she felt on the verge of crying. Blinking back tears one minute, then scrunching her fists in anger the next, her heart raced as her emotions ebbed and flowed.

Stepping into the doorway, Gary watched as the cascade of thoughts flittered across Candice's delicate features. He squinted at the wrinkles in her forehead, then chuckled when they disappeared. "Do you always torture yourself this way?" Sauntering into the room, he knelt beside her and retrieved the empty bottle, then toyed with it as she regained her connection to reality.

"I have no idea what I'm doing, baby." She sniffed, her

last thoughts tearing at her heart. "My life would have been so much easier if I had gone to school and gotten my degree before I had a family and so many other things to worry about."

"Yes, it would have," he agreed noncommittally. "But lingering on what happened with your father, your mother, and how Dakota was conceived won't help. Dwelling on those things you can't change isn't going to make today's choices easier."

She grimaced. "I know. And it only makes me unhappy."

"That's what your new medication is for, kitten."

"To help with the mood swings," she whispered, her bottom lip puckering as she sank deeper. She still hadn't accepted the little pink pills that made her feel…not herself.

"Perhaps it needs an adjustment."

"No. I just need time, baby. Please." She didn't move, as if the weight of the world held her in the chair.

"Let me take her," he offered, getting to his feet and holding his palms up before him.

Placing her bundle in his arms, Candy remained in the chair, watching as he carried her over to the crib and tucked her in. "I wouldn't have you guys. If things had been different then, they would be different now."

"Nope. Your whole life would have been changed. Focus on the good stuff, kitten." Straightening and admiring the sleeping toddler, he chuckled. "This is all good stuff."

"I don't want to quit school. But right now, it feels like that's the thing that makes everything so hard. Like if I would just stop fighting it, I would be happy, and things would get easier."

"Then you're on the right path."

Blinking a few times, Candy stammered, "But I just said everything is so hard. How can hard be the right path?"

"Because that's how life works," he whispered, turning and reaching for her hand. Clasping her fingers, he pulled her through the bathroom and shut the nursery door as they went. He wanted to make love to her and share the depths of his caring, but he could tell her mind was too jumbled to relax. Turning her away from him, he moved in behind and set to work.

"Trust me, kitten," he offered, rubbing her shoulders, then kneading them in a gentle massage. "When we get on the right path, life likes to test us. See if we're really committed."

"So I have to decide how badly I want to finish my degree."

"Exactly." He leaned in, first shoving her honey-colored hair to one side, then breathing warm puffs of air on her neck.

Finally catching on, Candy giggled. "It's Thursday."

"And I can't make love to my wife on Thursday?"

Biting her lip, she considered what the lost sleep would cost her. It had been a busy week and didn't look like it was going to be any better over the weekend. His tongue enticing as he toyed with her ear, she shivered. "You're a hard man to resist, Gerald Ford."

"Are you gonna purr for me?"

Turning to face him, she didn't bother to reply, her small frame taking over and leaving her troubled thoughts behind.

FIVE

Broken

THE FOLLOWING MORNING, Gary left for work early, passing Holly in her little, brown Civic as she approached their private drive. Giving her a wave, he grinned to himself as his thoughts wandered to his and Candy's night of togetherness. He loved his wife dearly and hated that she seemed easily defeated.

"She's stronger than she gives herself credit for," he spoke aloud to himself, using the drive to help him clear his thoughts. "We just have to keep supporting her and believing that she can do it."

Arriving at the brick building that was his home away from home, he parked in his usual spot and hurried to get around to the front of the fire station. The air had a bite to it, and he hoped it wasn't a sign they were in for a dismal winter. Coming around the corner, he noted the roll-up doors stood open, and their engines were both deployed.

"Great," he muttered. "A dismal beginning, in the least." Entering through one of the wide portals, he crossed to the meeting room that served as their kitchen as well. Inside, he set up the coffee pot for the guys when they returned, but he had hardly started the cycle when the first engine backed into its stall. *Perfect timing.*

Leaving the mess hall, he ran into Tom on his way over to his office. "Long night?" He only half-joked, concern crinkling his forehead as he inspected the crew as they unloaded their gear.

"Long, yes, but no fatalities, so I'd call it a win," Tom tossed back. Glancing through the glass wall, he could see the warm red glow. "Aw, honey. You shouldn't have."

"What? I made that for me," Gary countered, his face less grim. "Come by before you head out." He opened the door to his office and stepped inside.

"I'll take second shower." Catching the flat surface as his boss tried to close it against the cold, he joined him in the cubical and sealed it for himself. On the far wall, the baby box sat ready and waiting but unoccupied. Lifting the clipboard, he logged their return and replaced it on the hook. "What's up?"

"Oh, same old same old." Gerald took a seat and shuffled a few papers. "Anything happen that I should be aware of?"

"Naw. Like I said, it was busy with a few small fires, but property damage was the extent of it. But, and I hate to remind you again, my old lady is about to pop. Any day now, I'll be taking off for that."

"I know." Gary sighed. The mention of the impending birth amused him for a moment. Tom had been single the entire time he had known him, right up until February, when he suddenly got hitched. His wife came up pregnant almost immediately after, and Gerald had to wonder at what might have caused the suddenness of his transition from hard loving lady's man to family man in less than a year. "You have no idea what you're in for," he teased.

"Bah. It'll be great. I think that coffee's ready," he

observed, indicating the crew serving themselves. "It'll be gone quick with this cold snap."

"Yup, we better grab our mugs." Gary got to his feet and threw the door open, following the other man close behind. "I was just kidding about the baby. You'll enjoy it. Or most of it."

"Yeah, I will. You planning on adding another? Joy's a year now if my math's correct. We've had several more left in the box over the last year. Maybe you have room for another."

"That's not even funny, Tom," Gary shot back. He sometimes wished he had never mentioned that Joy was the first baby left in their haven, as his friend took an odd pleasure in reminding him of that fact.

Those in the break area cleared a path, allowing their two senior members to access the brew.

"Thanks, guys," Gary said with a nod as he located his favorite cup. A few of them snickered but didn't join the conversation. Most of those who worked under the pair were not family men and had no intention of joining them any time soon, so it was best to let the two old-timers alone.

Leaving them to their downtime, Gary and Tom served themselves and then returned to the front office, where they could talk again in private.

Slurping a large gulp, Tom grinned. "You do make a mean pot of java."

"Thanks." Gary chuckled, leaning back in his chair to enjoy his. His eyes flicking over at the light on the side of the box, he thought again of his daughter. He had pulled her out of it almost a year to the day. "I don't think we'll be having any more. At least not any time soon."

"Hey, man, I didn't mean to pry. If it's personal, I'd as soon not know."

"It's not that personal. We're in a hard spot right now. Candy's working to finish school, and her mother's health seems to be on a slow decline. We had to hire a nurse to see to her growing needs. I love Candy, and I wouldn't trade our lives together, but this year has been rough—the toughest one yet if I am being honest."

"Bummer."

"Yeah. We still have our fire…sometimes." His cheeks took on a warmer hue as he briefly thought of the previous night. "But families are hard work." Cutting his eyes over at the other man, he challenged, "Don't let that get in the way of your romance."

"Oh, trust me. We're never short on that!" Tom laughed loudly, insinuating his prowess.

"Yeah." Gary winced. Ever since he realized he was a rescuer, he had struggled with self-doubt. Things had always been a slow simmer between him and Candy. Glancing at the other man, he shoved the thoughts aside. "Ok. When the time comes, you call me. If you're on, I'll come and relieve you, and if you're off, I'll make sure the shifts are covered so you can be there. Sound good?"

"Sounds great, boss." Tom finished his cup and placed it on the desk. "Did I tell you she slipped up and spilled the news? We're having a boy." His grin said it all.

"That's great. Maybe you'll fare better than I have." Gary laughed loudly, thinking of his brood. "I'm the man of the house, quite literally. Dakota's got his issues, and we're surrounded by women."

"That rough?"

Gary chortled at the thought of it. "Heck yeah! Too much estrogen floating around. I miss the days when my life was simple," he confessed quietly, not bothering to mention the deeper problems they didn't discuss with anyone.

"Life is never simple," Tom pointed out. Wiping at his grimy face, he stood, ready for his turn in the shower. "Any time you think it is, that's when you're in the most danger of getting trounced."

Gary chuckled as his friend walked away. Alone, he muttered to himself, "Seems like lately, all we do is get trounced."

Arriving home that afternoon, Candy parked her car in the garage. Leaping out, she darted for the back door, the fifty yards seeming like a hundred with flurries of snow swirling around her as she ran. Stomping up to the entrance, she let the screen door slam shut behind her. "Son of a mother..."

Jolted by the bang, Holly glanced at the closed door leading to Lanelle's room. "Rough day?" she asked, hoping to hide her annoyance at the display. Rude as the action might have been, it was her house after all.

Cutting her eyes over at her, Candy pouted. "Is that coffee fresh?"

The nurse chuckled. "Yes. Would you like some?" Candy seemed to live in her own little world, something else she had discovered since becoming employed there, but she was getting used to it, and she hid her disapproval well, generally speaking.

Pulling at her hat and gloves, Candice grunted. "I'd love some, but I need to unpack. It's freezing, and it's starting to snow. It's too early for snow!" Not waiting for a reply, she darted down the hall to store her books in the office, then returned a few minutes later. "Ok, coffee and a sit."

"Mmhmm." Holly grinned knowingly. Picking up on Candy's previous observation, she added, "I know what you mean about the snow, although mother nature doesn't really care for our opinions." She pulled a clean mug out of the dishwasher and filled it for her, then topped off her own. "We can hate all we like, we're still going to get it."

"I see your point." Opening the fridge, Candy added a splash of creamer and shut the door with her foot as she reached for the sugar to add a spoon. Picking up the steaming brew, she carried it around to the back side and took a seat against the wall. "Where's Mom?"

Took her long enough. She'd been home at least ten minutes, and she only then noticed Lanelle wasn't present. "She decided to nap. She's been having one every afternoon while Joy sleeps." Holding her rebuke, she glanced at the back door, the loud slam still fresh in her mind as she glared accusingly at the panel of wood.

"Oh." Candy's lips puckered as she considered the news. "Glad I didn't wake her." Taking a sip, she directed the topic away from her careless blunder. "I bet that works out nicely for you girls. You and Carol were friends, so now you get to spend extra time together."

"Yes. Carol and I've known each other for years." Taking the chair opposite from her employer, Holly also sat. "We lost touch for a few years, and I went to work for Hospice, so I was surprised to hear from her when you guys were looking to hire someone. Although I must admit it's been nice coming back into each other's lives. I think the timing has been perfect."

"Oh, I agree. I'm glad she thought of you." Candy smiled at her genuinely. "What is a hospice nurse, exactly?"

"Well, we care for people coming to the end of their lives," the redhead explained while she stretched, unhurried. She and Candy had yet to become real friends, but she would like to if they were able. Sipping her coffee, she pondered a moment, then added, "We're there for them and for their families, too. Often, it's hard to say goodbye, so we act as nurse and as social worker much of the time."

The air caught in her chest, Candy felt sick—horrified that her fears of her mother's demise might be coming true. Huffing a few times, she searched for the right words before she finally blurted, "You took this job because you think my mother is dying?"

"No, I didn't take it because I think she's dying." Holly laughed anxiously at such an idea. After she had removed the shock from her voice, she said more quietly, "I needed a change, honestly. I don't think I realized it at the time, but I needed to get away from only treating the terminally ill. It was very draining. I was beginning to feel like the angel of death."

Candy features shifted to stricken. Holding her cup with both hands, she stared at her with wide eyes, easing the rim to her lips for a noisy sip.

"Not literally!" Holly exclaimed, noting her pallor and wishing she had never sat down with her. "It was just wearing on me. I needed to get away from it. That's all!"

Candy appeared unconvinced. Curling her tongue, she breathed deeply, also lowering her voice. "I'm sorry you weren't happy with your previous employment," she managed, simultaneously wondering if Gary would have hired the girl if "angel of death" had appeared on her resume. She could feel the twinge in the back of her mind, and she focused to remain in control.

"Oh, you have no idea how much I've enjoyed being in this house, sharing your good times," Holly confessed. "As I said, I needed the change, and this place has fit perfectly with my need to nurture." She giggled anxiously. *Getting to know Candice Ford will be harder than I thought.*

"You don't have a family of your own," Candy recalled from her interview. "But surely there will be one in the near future. A bright, successful young woman such as yourself should be quite a catch."

Holly stared at her, wondering how many insensitive comments and actions a person could make in a single afternoon. Glancing around, she considered bolting, at least until Lanelle was awake and needed her, but getting up and walking away might only make the situation worse. Licking her lips, she swallowed, searching for her most diplomatic self. "No, actually I don't see it that way. First, I would need a suitable partner, and I can't seem to find the right man. I worked my way through college, gaining my nursing degree while bouncing from one loser to the next. A very good friend of mine told me years ago that no one would ever love me like she did, and I've come to believe she was right. I've actually decided I'm going to swear off men," she finished in a huff.

Candy's eyes grew wide at her last statement. "Are you becoming a lesbian?"

"It doesn't work that way, Candy. One doesn't simply decide such a thing. When we fall in love, it's with a person, not a physique, or it shouldn't be." Holly's words squeaked loudly, her face flushed. Ratcheting her voice down a few notches, she said more calmly, "Perhaps we aren't ready for this conversation."

"What conversation?" Carol asked, entering the kitchen from the living room.

"Holly thinks she might be gay," Candy grunted, unable to take her eyes off their newest member and catching the glance the other two women shared. "What?"

"There's nothing wrong with her being gay," Carol soothed, helping herself to a cup of the coffee.

"I never said there was." Candice pushed her face into her hands, embarrassed by the whole situation.

"No, but your reaction speaks volumes." Carol took the empty seat at the end of the table so they formed a little triangle between them. Seeing the girl's frown, she sighed.

"Candy, I'm going to be real blunt with you." Holly paused, tapping the table a few times with the tips of her fingers. "I think you have a hard time with empathy. You don't see things from other people's points of view, which makes you very hard to get to know and to trust on a personal level."

"I agree," Carol seconded, leaning her forehead against her hands as she clasped them before her.

Candy's gut ached as if she had been punched. Gasping for air, she managed, "You don't think I care about other people?"

"It's not that you don't care."

Carol shrugged, looking at Holly dolefully, silently begging her not to do this now.

"Maybe it's your birth control," Holly reasoned. "You may not be tolerating it well."

Candy gaped at her, surprised she had hit so close to her inner battle and the medication she took in secret out of fear at what others would think. "It's not that. My meds are fine," she snapped, on the edge of losing it.

"Well, something is off. From what I've seen, you have a hard time seeing beyond your own problems. I think something happened to you, and you are broken by it some-how. You have some healing to do from old wounds, and your life won't ever get easier until you face that pain and deal with it." Her heart racing, Holly could see she had struck a nerve. "I'm sorry, Candy. You and I don't know each other that well, but I'd really like to. I love your family and caring for your mother, and I think we could all benefit."

"If you could change me," Candy finished for her, anger seeping into her words. "You think I'm broken. That there's something wrong with me. That I need to be fixed. Is that what hospice nurses do? Fix people?" She blinked rapidly, hot tears spilling over to streak down her cheeks.

"I didn't say that. I think you could learn to be a little more understanding if you wanted to. Plus, I think you would benefit if you did. Things wouldn't always be such a struggle." Holly's eyes teared as well. "You are so young, and I hate to think of you running yourself ragged this way."

"We both do," Carol quickly agreed.

Wiping at her drops of sorrow, Candy glanced between them. They had already talked about her and her condition; she was certain of it. "So you're teaming up against me on this?" The thought occurred to her that she could fire the pair of them on the spot, but then where would she be? Besides, if she did that, she would have to explain why to Gary. No, she had to stick it out until she could figure out what to do about this plan of theirs.

Giggling anxiously, the two girls shared another glance. They were on thin ice, and they knew it. Enjoying their coffee for a few minutes, they let Candy calm down before Carol confessed, "We have spoken of it. I know Cathy is your best friend, but we're practically part of your family, and we only want what's best for you."

"Wow." Candy forced a smile. "I know you guys mean well, but I really don't think this is a problem. I love my family and do all I can for them. I have my friends, like you said, and I think they all love me the way I am."

Her jaw dropping slightly, Holly gaped at her. *She has no*

clue. She couldn't believe anyone could be that dense, that far out of touch with socially acceptable behavior.

Seeing the other woman's reaction, Carol covered quickly, "Well, you know there is always room for improvement." Candy was their employer after all. Starting such a campaign would be foolish if the girl was resistant to the idea. "Let's table this discussion for now. I can see you are both very passionate about your point of view, and pushing on from here wouldn't be good for any of us."

"Always the sensible one," Candy observed with a click of her tongue. Her jaw tight, bitterness boiled below the surface, coupled with a deep hurt. She'd been working on herself for years, since she and Gary had started dating in fact. Having these two smug little witches pointing out she wasn't perfect bruised her ego significantly, and all she wanted to do was run upstairs and cry.

Not willing to give them the satisfaction, Candice forced herself to finish the drink. When she was done, she washed out her cup and returned it to the dishwasher before excusing herself to the office where she would study the afternoon away and could sulk in private.

SIX

Winter's Wonder

SATURDAY MORNING, Candy slept in. Gary by her side, she curled herself into the crook of his arm and inhaled deeply to enjoy his scent. Her fingers trailing the hairs on his chest as he slept, she turned the previous afternoon in her thoughts for the umpteenth time. She was less angry, but the way Holly had spoken to her still stung. Part of her wanted to blurt the whole thing to him and announce they both needed to be let go.

However, fear that he would take their side prevented her from doing so. Besides, if she succeeded in running them both off, they would have to be replaced, and as distasteful as having them want to fix her might be, having to adjust to a new set of caregivers loomed as a much greater challenge.

Her fingers pulling at a few of the curls, she grinned deviously. They had accused her of lacking empathy for others as if she were completely self-absorbed. *I'm not. I'm just...busy.* Realizing she had nothing to do that morning, it would be the perfect opportunity to prove them wrong. Sliding up to reach his mouth, she pressed her lips to his, waking him with the intent of making love. *After all, it shouldn't always be him kindling our fire.*

Downstairs a short time later, Carol placed Joylana in her highchair and greeted Holly as she came in with a breeze of cold air. "Good morning! Coffee's fresh."

"Thanks." Pulling off her coat and fluffing her short red locks, the nurse grinned at her friend. "I hope you're not still miffed at me."

"No." Carol sighed. "I forgive you. But please, do not antagonize Candy. I don't know her whole story, but she's been through a lot. You really struck a nerve with her, and you win more bees with honey...or something like that."

"Hey, you said you agreed with me and she needed to learn a few social graces," Holly hissed. "Her bitch-switch is set at eight-point-five most of the time, and I'm sorry, but there's no reason for that, and if there is, she should give it." Helping herself to the coffee, she glanced at Lanelle's door, hoping to let her client sleep a little longer.

Carol exhaled loudly, thinking maybe Candy wasn't ready to give it. "Yes, she does struggle with her temper, but I really do think it has to do with her birth control. She has always been edgy, but this depth only started after she and Gary decided to adopt rather than conceive." Staring at her hands, she swallowed, hoping she hadn't shared more than she should have about Candy's private choices. "And I do agree with you, but a frontal assault is obviously not the answer." Her voice tinkled, and she glanced at the other woman slyly. "We need to be covert in our efforts. If we want to help her, to really change her, we need to do it with love."

"With love," Holly echoed. She leaned her rear end against the counter and smiled behind her cup. "I love when you talk that way."

Her face flushed a soft pink, Carol returned to getting Joy situated. Adding a chopped banana to the tray, she hummed to herself. "I'll have breakfast ready shortly if you want to get Lanelle lined out. I'll go bring Daks down afterwards, if he doesn't stumble in before then."

"Fine," Holly teased, agreeing to the neutrality of food. "I'll play nice with Candy, but be aware that I'm not pleased with her typical behavior. I think it's a disgrace that a grown woman can be so oblivious to others, especially those she claims to care so much about."

"Give her time, love," Carol whispered as she passed behind the chair and reached for the door. "We'll mold her into a better person. I promise."

Opening the portal, Holly entered the dark room. Making it to the bedside, she switched on the lamp, then turned her attention to her charge. "Lanelle, it's time to wake up, sweetie."

"Breakfast?"

"Soon. Let's have a bath today and put on some fresh pajamas. I'm sure you won't be going out since we have a fresh layer of snow!" She made the announcement as if the older woman were a child and she was enticing her to get up and go play.

"Snow," Lanelle slurred. "Daks loves snow."

"Yes. I'm sure he does," Holly agreed, pulling back the covers and encouraging her to move. "That's it." Taking her arms, she helped her to sit, then stand to make her way into her private bath. Thankfully, this part of the old house had been renovated and was perfect for accommodating an elderly person. She had been in many homes that weren't, and that made the job of caregiver more difficult in the end.

Half an hour later or so, they had accomplished the bath

and were in the process of applying the warm flannel when Dakota's unmistakable laugh carried through the air. Pausing, the two women gazed at each other with wide eyes and matching grins. Completing the task, Holly followed as Lanelle hurried out to greet him in her slow and sliding gait. Seeing her into her favorite chair, she returned to the chamber to tidy it before she joined the meal.

Making up the bed, Holly sighed deeply. It was true she wanted to help Candy grow and become a better person, but in the end, that wasn't why she was there. Furthermore, and more importantly, it terrified her that she might be asked to leave. "I'll just have to keep my opinions to myself," she scolded as she fluffed the pillow and dropped it into place.

It's not like I've never been wrong before. Since working together, she had discovered Caroline's life had not been the easy one she had always imagined. On the contrary, Carol had suffered her own hardships through high school and had also endured a few poor relationships in the romance department. Her jaw tight, Holly frowned as she recalled the blonde's doleful expression when she confessed what she had done to Gary a few years ago when they dated. *No wonder Candy doesn't trust us.*

Satisfied with the bedroom, she turned to the bath and straightened it as well. She had discovered a happiness in that house, one that she had longed for and that hospice had never fulfilled. Caring for Lanelle came easily, and having her dear friend Carol back in her life after all these years had moved her, changed her in ways she had never expected. She had tried to talk to Candy about these things, but the girl wasn't ready to know yet. *Maybe in a few weeks or months, I can explain it and be open about it. Maybe by Christmas, we'll be in a better place.* Until then, she would do her best not to upset anyone with her thoughts and opinions.

"Mamamam," Joylana called, and Holly paused to wave at her through the doorway.

Out in the kitchen, the noise of breakfast had grown louder. Dakota took his seat next to his sister, who had finished her meal but was content to bang on the plastic tray and babble at him just the same. Lanelle's room tidy, Holly joined them, serving a plate for herself and one for their grandmother. Taking her seat against the wall, beside the older woman, she sighed. "What a perfect day."

"Perfect," Daks mimicked. Pointing at the back door, his intentions were clear.

"We can't go outside until Mommy is up and says it's ok," Carol soothed. "Eat your pancakes, and we'll see in a bit."

Holding out her hand, Joylana looked up at her with wide dark eyes, silently begging for one of them. Curling her fingers a few times, she added a grunt, in case her desire wasn't clear.

"Do you want a pancake?" Candy cooed as she entered the room. Freshly showered, her skin practically glowed.

Holly glanced at their matron, considering if she still appeared angry. Thankfully, she seemed more relaxed than usual, and it was probably all but forgotten if she let it go on her end. "Good morning."

"Good morning, everyone," Candice sang in reply, picking a small round morsel from the stack and handing it to her daughter. "Did everyone see the snow outside?"

"I did, firsthand," Holly grumbled. "I can't believe it came so early this year."

"I told you yesterday I saw flurries." Candy laughed, choosing to ignore the rest of the unpleasant conversation. "Looks like Roger and Eve didn't get away in time this year."

"I'll be taking them to the airport this afternoon," Gary

reminded her as he joined them. Serving himself a cup of warm brew, he leaned against the counter and surveyed the group of females, recalling what he had said about them the day before. "All that estrogen," he mumbled, his body still tingling from his wife's morning gift.

"You be careful," Candy warned. Taking her seat at the table next to Daks, her features lost a bit of their shine. "The roads may be bad if they haven't run the plows yet."

"Oh, it's not that bad, at least not yet," Holly countered. "If we get more, then we can worry."

"I still worry," Candice confessed. "He has the weekend off, and then he goes back on nights." She really hated his rotating shift, which took another half notch off her mood.

Of course, that meant the house would need to be quieter so he could sleep during the day, but they had grown accustomed to the alternating schedule. Only Holly would have to adapt, but since Lanelle was confined to the first floor, it would be an easy adjustment.

"Nights aren't so bad. But as the weather gets colder, it may be more difficult for Holly to make it in every day." Gary grinned at their new nurse, fairly certain she wouldn't have any problem, considering her independent personality.

"I can drive in just about anything." Holly cut a few bites for Lanelle, then had a few for herself.

"I hadn't thought of that," Candy breathed. "Our winter wonderland can be so treacherous."

"We'll make do," Carol offered, finally ready to sit with her own plate. "Even if she misses a day, we'll get by." She smiled encouragingly. Sensing Candy's collapsing spirits, she did her best to prop her friend's mood and help her focus on the light.

Grinning at them, Gary heaped eggs and bacon onto his plate. He might have downplayed the dynamics of their household to Tom, but in the end, he really enjoyed the crowd of women and the way they had come together as a harmonious family unit. Candy really needed their support even if she couldn't bring herself to say so, and their willingness to provide it indicated this coming winter might not be so dismal after all.

SEVEN

The Miles Between

EIGHT WEEKS LATER...

"Say goodbye to Grandmother," Candy encouraged sweetly. Grasping Joylana's hand, she waved it at the screen.

Their weekly conference call coming to an end, it had become a fair tradeoff, something to lessen the miles between them, and Eve had said nothing more about her disappointment at being relegated to Florida for the winter. Smiling into the camera, she gave no hint of the sadness within. "Let her walk for me again before you go." she pleaded, folding her hands and pressing her fingers to her lips.

Rolling her eyes, Candice moved to comply. "Come on, baby girl. Grandmother wants to see...one more time." She knelt a few feet from the sofa and helped Joy get her legs under her, taking care that they were still in view of the camera. Glancing at Gary, she noticed he grinned from ear to ear at the spectacle.

Almost as if she knew the importance of the task, Joy clapped her hands a few times, then left the safety of her mother's arms. Taking wobbly steps, she lumbered forward to close the distance, squealing happily when she reached her father's knees and he scooped her up. "Dadadada."

"Oh, she is so precious!" Eve declared, wiping at an escaped tear. "We'll call again Christmas morning if that's all right."

"Not too early," Candy blurted, slightly annoyed that her mother-in-law insisted on being part of everything they did. "Enjoy your holiday there in the sunshine," she added, twisting the invisible knife.

Watching her, Gary became thoughtful, wondering if his wife knew how her remarks sounded. The doctor may have adjusted her dose, but she still had difficulty with her sensitivity to others. He only hoped they would find the right balance soon, as he felt certain they wouldn't be able to hide the cause of her unpredictable mood swings and thoughtless comments forever.

"We'll make it later in the day," Roger assured, reaching to disconnect. "Bye, everyone." The screen went black.

"Well, that was fun." Not letting his concern over Candy drag him down, Gary raised Joy above his head and zoomed her in the air, laughing with her as she cackled. Chewing on her pudgy fingers, her happiness filled the room.

"Yeah, fun," Candy echoed, getting up to clear away the equipment. She dreaded their weekly call and honestly wished she could bow out of more of them, but since the school semester had ended a few weeks prior, she no longer had that excuse. On a happy note, she had made two As and two Bs, which was a vast improvement over the year before, she recalled silently to herself, which improved her mood. *I guess spending a few minutes sharing with them isn't so bad.*

Everything put away, she left her husband and children to join the girls in the kitchen. Plunking into the chair across from her mother, she exhaled loudly. "Another week down. But they're going to call again on Wednesday. Are we all set for the Christmas dinner?" It would only be their small group since Gary's family had all been over for their traditional Halloween feast. That and Candy didn't have any other family to speak of.

"We are," Carol calmly agreed. "It will be a pleasant day."

"Are you sure you don't want to bring a date?" Candy asked casually. "We really don't mind if either of you wants to invite a fellow over," she teased, glancing between her and Holly, who was busy washing a few dishes. Holly had never said anything else about giving up men, so there was still hope for her to have a family as far as Candy knew.

"No. We're perfectly happy with just us," Carol assured.

"Uh-huh," Candice grunted. Curling her tongue, she contemplated how she might improve the situation, knowing it was unlikely that either of the girls would find a good man hiding in her kitchen.

"We're still on for the winter carnival tomorrow, right?" Gary asked as he joined them, placing Joy into her highchair so they could eat.

"Sure. It sounds like fun," Holly agreed. Drying her hands on a towel, she dropped it over the edge of the sink and reached for a pair of plates, one for her and one for Lanelle as usual. She had gotten so used to caring for the other woman it was like second nature these days. "We'll take the wheelchair, and I'll push her around to make it easier. You said it's indoors, right?"

"Some of it is." Candy got to her feet, gathering Dakota's serving as well as her own. "I've heard there's a path that wanders through the gardens that will be lighted. You may be able to make it through, but we'll have to see." Thinking of the lights, her mind leapt to the previous year. *Benjamin!* He had gone with them last year, with he and Carol appearing quite cozy in their seat while sharing a blanket. *I'll invite Ben.*

Deciding to play the role of matchmaker, Candy clicked her tongue and glanced between the two women. As far as she knew, Carol and Ben still dated on occasion, and even if they were no longer a thing, he might be a good match for Holly. Grinning to herself, she kept the idea a secret, hoping it would make a pleasant surprise for at least one of their housemaids.

Seeing her devious expression, Gary made his way over and leaned in. "What are you up to?"

"I'm planning a surprise," she whispered back. It had been a few months since Holly had joined them, and over that time, things had settled into a pleasant routine. "I'd like to do something nice for the girls, or at least one of them, if I can."

"Oh, brother," Gary replied, laughing quietly. He knew his wife, and any time she did anything nice, it always held the potential to turn into a real disaster.

"Hello," a deep male voice greeted her when the call connected.

"Hey, Ben! It's Candice Ford. How are you?"

"Hi, Candy. I'm good. It's a little late for a call though, don't you think?" After ten on a Saturday night, Ben glanced at the clock anxiously and wondered what calamity could have prompted her to connect.

"I'm sorry to reach out so late. I honestly only thought of inviting you earlier this evening."

"Inviting me?" He hesitated, not sure where this was leading.

"Yes. When was the last time you spoke to Carol?"

His chest tight, he grimaced. "It's been a while. What's all this about, Mrs. Ford?"

The formality of his voice startled her. They were friends, at least she thought they were, unless something had happened that she wasn't aware of. Biting her lip, she changed tactics. "Actually, I'm not really calling about Carol. I think if things were going well between you, we would have heard about it."

Silence.

"We have a nurse here who is caring for my mother. Holly. I'd like to introduce you to her tomorrow...if you'd be willing. We're going to the winter carnival, and that's the reason I called—to invite you." Her words tumbled over each other by the end.

"Well, that's really sweet of you, I guess," he stammered, his thoughts racing. If she were calling to invite him to meet Holly, then she had no clue what was going on in her own house, and he certainly didn't want to be the one to break it to her.

"Look, Candy," he sidestepped, "I've already got plans for tomorrow. And you're right. Things didn't exactly work out between me and Carol." Thinking back, they had held hands beneath the blanket the night he had joined them on their light-seeing quest. He had even gotten a few kisses from her over the next few weeks when they had dated. But things had fizzled quickly. "I actually think Caroline is seeing someone," he mumbled.

"But I want you to meet Holly. Forget Carol." Candy laughed anxiously, seizing the opportunity. "Come with us, and let's see how it goes."

"I really can't. But thank you for thinking of me." He

winced, then added, "I'll talk to you later." He clicked the end button before she could say anything else.

Staring at the phone, Candy sighed. "Well, that was a little rude." Putting it on the charger, she shut off the office light and slowly made her way up the stairs.

"You look a little sad," Gary pointed out when she joined him. "Was talking to my mother that bad?"

"Yeah, I'm a little sad, and no it's not because of your mother. Ben's busy tomorrow."

"Ben? You called him at this hour?"

"Yeah. I wanted to try and set him up with Holly."

"Oof," Gary grunted, not seeing the logic behind it. "Didn't he date Carol for a while?"

"So did you," she clipped, angry for a moment. "He might have had better luck with Holly."

Coughing a short laugh, Gary shook his head. "I doubt that." Glancing at his wife, he let it go. "We need to get some sleep." Raising his eyebrows at her, his lips formed a tantalizing pucker.

"Oh, Gary." She grinned, understanding exactly what he meant. Sliding beneath the covers, she scooted to the middle of the bed and waited for him to join her, certain sleep was the last thing on his mind.

EIGHT

Making Do

CATCHING giggles floating up from the kitchen as she came down the stairs, Candy sighed. Carol and Holly got along fabulously, and she should be grateful, but having missed the opportunity to fix one of them up with Ben had her perturbed. Standing side by side at the stove, the two girls were whispering and then bumping their hips together playfully, a funny sight with Caroline still in her pajamas.

"Good morning," Candy sang, announcing her presence, startling the pair and sending them into peals of laughter.

"Good morning," Holly eventually replied, her smile broad as she made plates and prepared for their breakfast routine.

Sitting in her chair, Lanelle had been watching them, a silly grin decorating her features.

"Well, you look pleased," Candy observed as she poured her coffee and took her seat across from her. Catching Joylana smiling at her, she decided to play with her for a moment. Earning a few "mamamas" would put her in a better mood.

Paying her no mind, Holly brought their plates around

and took her seat next to her charge. "We're just getting warmed up for winter carnival day, aren't we, Mimi?"

"It'll be fun," Lanelle agreed in her scraggly voice.

"Yes, it will," Caroline seconded as she set a place for Dakota and presented Candy with a serving for Joylana. "Daks, breakfast," she called into the front room, where he played with his firetruck in front of the Christmas tree.

Accepting the smaller meal, Candice continued to play with her daughter, scooping bites of egg and biscuit for her as she considered the possibilities.

"Good morning, kitten." Gary kissed her lightly on the cheek as he passed by, then gave their daughter a fond pat on the shoulder as well. Crossing to the back door, he parted the curtain and peeked outside. "More snow. You think they will still hold the event?"

"I'm sure they will, but if they cancel, I guess we can do the lights again this year." Finishing off the plate, Candy stood to collect some for herself.

"Go play snow," Dakota suggested, then bit off a large chunk of bacon.

"Uhuh," Carol redirected, reminding him to chew with his mouth closed.

"Our mornings are always chaos," Gary grumbled jokingly as he glanced around to see that everyone had been fed. The last to fix his plate, he helped himself to the remainders, dumping them into a large pile and taking an empty seat at the far end of the table.

"A lot of mouths to feed," Candy seconded. Her mood restored, she cajoled her son, "Don't worry, baby. We'll get to play in the snow. Mommy's off for two more weeks."

"What time does the carnival begin?" Holly inquired, still taking turns with Lanelle for bites of the delicious food.

"At noon. We'll have time to clean up and get everyone

dressed. I suggest layers since we may be outside part of the time," Candy advised.

"You seem pretty chipper about this outing," Gary observed, happy she hadn't let Ben's refusal to join them spoil their day.

"Oh, I am." Her words came out airily, almost whimsical. "It's going to be a fun day. We should take the stroller. That way if Joy falls asleep, she won't be dead weight on anyone's arm."

"Hmmp," Gary grunted. "Ok. As soon as I'm done, I'll get that loaded in the back of the Suburban, as well as the wheelchair. Any other big stuff that has to go?"

"Firetruck," Dakota declared, earning a laugh from the others.

"No, silly, we won't need the firetruck," Gerald teased. At least he hoped they wouldn't. Then he added thoughtfully, "Do you think Santa will be there?"

"Santa!" his son squealed, obviously not too old yet for the holiday tradition.

"If he is, we should get some pictures of the kids with him." Candy grinned dreamily at the thought of it. "Man, this is going to be a big day!"

"I'll pack extra clothes for both of them, then." Carol got to her feet and started gathering up the dishes. "That way if anyone gets messy, we can still get some nice shots of them in their fresh clothes."

"And I guess that means neither of you decided to bring a date today," Candy observed with a crooked grin as another idea occurred to her. "You know, I bet there are some eligible guys at the firehouse. Who knows? Maybe Gary can set you up with a couple of them!"

A look of disbelief flittered across Holly's features before she managed to swipe it away. "Thanks, but no thanks. In case I didn't mention it, I'm seeing someone."

"You are?" Carol gasped, earning a dark glance from her friend and co-worker.

"Yes, silly, I am," Holly snapped, then soothed, "So again, thanks, but no thanks."

Cutting her a crooked grin, Carol teased, "Well, I'm spoken for as well, so I guess all those firehouse hotties will just have to do without."

Surprised, Candy gaped at her. "I didn't realize either of you were dating. And here I was suggesting you bring them to Christmas dinner, but maybe we should have given you the day off!"

"It's quite all right." Holly laughed as if she had gotten away with a trick on someone. "I'll be here, happy to share the day with my adoptive family."

Caroline only grinned at her, equally pleased to spend the day at the Ford residence.

"Ok, everybody out," Gary called once they found a place to park along the row of handicapped spots. Hanging the tag in the window of the Suburban, he thumped it with his thumb, then rolled out the driver side door.

Crunching through the snow to the back, he pulled out the stroller, then the wheelchair.

Taking command of the stroller, Candy called, "Dibs on Joy."

"I've got Daks," Carol replied, locating the small bag she had packed for him and tossing it over her shoulder.

"I've got Lanelle," Holly chimed in, giggling at their silliness.

Beaming, Gerald couldn't have been happier, again

marveling at how their oversized family made do in every situation. "Everyone has their phone? We'll text when we locate Santa and get those pictures early if we're able."

Once everyone had paired up and was ready to explore, the group entered through the front of the glass doors. Inside, a magical wonderland spread before them, complete with sections of winter scenes, food and craft booths, and even a few live-action skits to enjoy.

"Wow, this is amazing," Candy breathed, enchanted with excitement buzzing in the air. "I can't believe this is our first year to come here!"

"I don't think they've been putting this on very long. This is like the third year, maybe," Carol informed her. "At any rate, I'm sure it doesn't change much from year to year, so let's enjoy it all while it's shiny and new."

"Hear, hear," Lanelle seconded, holding up her arms while Holly adjusted the blankets across her lap.

"Ok, if everyone has their carnival buddy, we are headed outside to check out the gardens." Looping his arm around Candy's shorter shoulders, he gave her a nudge to lead the way.

"Bye, guys," she called to the rest as they headed out the south doors and into the chilly patio beyond.

"Which way are we going?" Carol asked, cutting her eyes over at Holly as she held firmly to Dakota's hand.

"Want see horses," he informed her, pulling at her arm to urge her over to the north entrance. They had passed the arena on the way in, and he had not forgotten about the giant beasts.

"You only have twenty dollars," she reminded him gently as they cleared the door, Lanelle's chair following as Holly pushed her along. "If you spend it all riding, you won't be able to get or do anything else "

"I know," he sang, as if it were enough to buy the whole place if he desired it.

"Don't you worry," Lanelle called after him. "Mimi's got money, too."

"Oh, you're going to spoil him," Holly informed her, laughing despite her rebuke.

"It's what grandmother's do," she slurred, overjoyed to be spending the afternoon out, despite the cold.

Across the way, in the back garden, Gary pulled Candy close as she pushed the stroller in front of her. Inside it, Joylana babbled and pointed at the decorations lining the walk.

"Pretty, aren't they?" Candy scanned the crowd teaming around them. Joy had been part of their family for a year, and either people had gotten used to their mixed-race family or she had gotten better at ignoring the stares. Pulling up in front of a scene of elves frolicking in the snow, she paused and turned the wheels so she could crouch down next to her daughter.

Taking the other side, Gary joined her. "Daddy's girl likes the snow, I think."

"Yes, she does," Candy agreed. Stealing a kiss from her husband across the top of the stroller when they stood, she sighed. She couldn't have asked for a more perfect day.

NINE

What a Girl Needs

PUSHING Lanelle in her wheelchair turned out to be hard work, especially on the uneven stones of the outdoor path. The constant jarring of the rough terrain was enough to make the older woman's teeth rattle.

"Let's park," her charge offered after they had made it to the carrousel.

"But there's so much to see," Holly countered, disappointed she had let her down.

"I'll see plenty," Lanelle assured. Raising her hand, she indicated a good spot. "Over there, out of the way."

"Out of the way," Holly puffed under her breath. "You are never in the way, love." Obediently maneuvering the large wheels, she soon had her tucked away on a part of the path where others could pass by easily while Lanelle still had full view of the musical contraption. "How's this?"

"It's fine."

Holly knelt beside her, adjusting the blanket across her lap. "It may be too cold out here." Clasping her hands, she tested her fingers. "Keeping you warm is of utmost importance."

"It's fine," Lanelle insisted, a bit more loudly.

"Ok." Standing, Holly pulled her hat down to cover her ears and looked around, admiring the throng of people milling about. "I didn't realize so many would come."

A hand goosed her, and she spun around, facing Carol squarely.

"Boo."

"Boo yourself," Holly snapped, her eyes darting around a bit wildly.

"Relax." Carol stepped closer, her fingers reaching and entwining with the other girl's gloved digits.

Even through the knit material, Holly could feel her warmth. "This doesn't scare you?" she whispered, hoping the noise of the crowd would hide the tremor in her voice, her heart thumping loudly in her ears.

"No. I'm growing tired of hiding. Aren't you?"

Pulling away, Holly wasn't ready for such a bold confession, especially out in the open of a snowy, winter plaza. Searching for a distraction, she smacked her hands together anxiously. "Dakota, did you get to ride the horses?"

"No." His lip stuck out in a small pout.

"Oh, no. What happened?"

"The guy said he wasn't covered by the insurance," Carol explained. "They were letting other kids ride, though."

"'Normal kids,'" Holly spat quietly toward Carol as she nodded. "Damn it." She knelt beside Daks, placing her hand on his shoulder to get his attention, eager to make amends. "Do you want to ride these horses?" It was too fine a day for one of them to be disappointed.

"We should ask before you offer," Caroline pointed out, leaving them to speak with the attendant. She grinned widely when she returned, taking his hand. "Let's go, little man. We have horses to tame."

"Yeah!" he whooped, eagerly following her.

People standing in the line moved over, allowing them to pass.

"They're letting him cut," Lanelle observed.

"Of course they are. As hard as he tries to be like everyone else, he never will be." Her voice held a hint of sadness, dragging at her mood. Prophetic, in fact, even if the older woman didn't understand the meaning behind them, as she was only half speaking of him.

"It's ok. He is loved."

Loved. The word echoed in her mind. She had loved Caroline once. Through the years of struggle, her feelings had slipped into the background. But being close to her again over the last few months, the fire had been rekindled, ready to burst out of control and consume her in the conflagration. *I should have known it would happen.* But they weren't teenagers, and if she wasn't careful, it wouldn't be a man who broke her heart this time.

"Yes, he is loved," she breathed, no longer watching the boy. She had become fixated with the blond hair framing Caroline's lovely face. Watching it flick in the wind, her mind wandered, drifting back in time. Years melted away, and she gasped, air caught in her lungs and refusing to allow another breath.

"Carol," she whispered. "Carol, we can't do this," her fourteen-year-old-self resisted.

"Who will know?" Caroline's hand started at her hip, tracing her waist, barely brushing the side of her breast. "Oh God, I touched you!" The blonde giggled, making another grab.

Holly stepped back, preventing the second feel. "I said no."

"But you want to," Carol insisted, her lip forming a small pout. "I know you do. Why can't we just be who we are?"

"Because." Holly stood tall, imposing her height. "People won't like who we are. I know you don't want to hear that, but it's not ok."

"How can it not be ok? I love you, Holly. You're my best friend. No one will ever love you as much as I do."

The words faded, echoing in her mind as the memory disappeared. Before her, a carousel whizzed by, her best friend spinning around as she clung to the side of a carved wooden horse. Tears forced her to blink as she recalled all that moment in time had cost them. Laughing, Carol and Daks both were obviously enjoying the ride, and Holly coughed a giggle as well, carried by their boisterous song out of the darkness of the past.

Smiling, the tears dampened her lashes. *Caroline.* She had always been so carefree. *No, she didn't care, not then and not now.* If Holly could let go of her fears, she knew Carol would be waiting for her. *If.* It was a big word with so much at stake. The ride slowly grinding to a stop, she wiped at her eyes, removing the droplets.

"That was amazing!" Carol stumbled to them, giddy as she held Dakota's hand.

"Ride again!" He pulled at her arm, hoping for another turn.

"I'll take you in a few minutes," Holly offered, caught up in her friend's glee. "Be patient, Daks." She wasn't talking to him. She could feel the tug from within. *Take the chance,* her younger self breathed.

"Sit with Mimi," his grandmother offered. "Let's watch the ride."

He clambered onto her lap, really too old for it, but his

mind was forever young despite the size of his growing body. "T'anks, Mimi," he purred, content for the moment.

Stepping closer to her, Holly sized up Caroline. "You know, I used to be taller than you."

"Yeah, when we were kids," Carol shot back, amused by her friend's teasing. Searching her soft green orbs, she waited. Their relationship had grown in the few months Holly had worked in the Ford household, and Carol wanted more. Much more. But so far, they seldom had more than a few stolen minutes alone together, and Holly wasn't ready for their relationship to be public. Carol knew this. She accepted this. When the other woman didn't act, she took a step back, not wanting to make her would-be girlfriend uncomfortable. Glancing at their charges, she could see they were still engrossed in the glittering, noisy distraction, probably oblivious to the sexual tension sparking between them.

Holly could sense her pulling away, probably on her account. Caroline was protective of her and always had been, so it didn't surprise her when she turned her back on her to prevent her from doing anything stupid—anything she might regret.

Carol had kissed her several times in the last few weeks, but each one left her the same way—breathless. Suddenly, the carnival and the crowd didn't matter. She needed her— needed to feel the softness of her lips and the warmth of her hands. Stepping up behind her, she threw her arms around her, pushing her wool cap aside and breathing against her neck.

"Caroline," she whispered, nuzzling her ear. "Remember when—?"

"Shh," Carol cut her off. Pushing her face around, she found her mouth, her lips parting as she tasted her.

Holly moaned, opening herself to the moment, not giving

a damn what anyone around them might think.

"Shit." Candice gasped for air. "Shit, shit." Within her mind and body, a surge of adrenaline had her fighting for control.

"What's the matter?" Gary asked, struggling to adjust the straps of the stroller. Kneeling, his back to them, he hadn't seen a thing.

But Candy had. She had seen it all.

Across the open patch of ground, maybe fifty feet between them, there could be no mistake. Not with her mother and son sitting right beside them.

Shit. How could she not have known? *How could they do this to me? To US?*

"I think that's it." Gary stood, puzzled. "What are you on about?"

"Nothing!" Candy's gaze snapped to meet his. The kiss had ended. *Maybe they won't do it again. Maybe he won't notice if they do. Shit.*

"Let's go find something to snack on," she suggested, pushing her hand through the loop of his arm and guiding him towards the row of stands at the end. "I bet they've got some really good stuff that's just awful for us."

"Oh, you want awful!" He laughed, enjoying her playful mood. It had been a while since she had been this happy. "Ok. Let's go find something awful."

Glancing back, Candy couldn't see them anymore. *Maybe they went back to the main building.* She hoped they had. *And that they stopped whatever the hell that was.* Forcing the image from her mind, she focused. They needed this day, she and Gary—needed to be together and carefree for a few hours. *Shit.*

TEN

Oblivious

ROLLING THROUGH THE DARKNESS, Gary contemplated their near-perfect day. *We stayed at the carnival longer than intended, but everyone had a great time.* Candy had thrown a mini tantrum she refused to explain, but she seemed to calm down, and they had shared a pleasant afternoon and evening.

Glancing at her through the shadows, he wondered again if she should have her meds adjusted since things had declined on the ride home. *She resisted the suggestion before, but the evidence seems clear that we have still not found the right dose.* He would choose the right time to suggest it when they were alone, but he knew tonight probably wouldn't be it since Candy hadn't said a word—a good indicator she was upset. *Perhaps more than upset.*

"I'll get Joy," he announced when they were safely parked behind the house, freeing her to disappear inside and hide in the office or upstairs if that's what she needed to do.

Instead, Candice exited the vehicle and slammed the door. A massive wave rocked the heavy-duty Suburban, surprising everyone inside.

"Candy, what is wrong with you?" Lanelle managed to sputter.

"Nothing. Everything." She stomped up the steps and unlocked the back door, the screen smacking the frame behind her. Inside, she dropped to her knees, clenching her gloved fists as she screamed, then ground her teeth furiously.

Following, holding Dakota's hand, Carol gasped. "Candy!" Quickly recovering herself, she pulled him along towards the stairs and removed his coat. "Go play in the den, sweetheart. I'll draw your bath in a few minutes."

"You'll do no such thing." Candy panted, getting to her feet.

The rest of the family had made it inside, but the happy mood of the day was gone, evaporated into bewilderment and rage. Cuddling his daughter against his chest, Gary considered his options. "I need to unload everything," he dared cautiously.

Pulling off her gloves, Candy dropped them and her jacket to the floor. "I'll take her." Holding up her hands, she waited, but Joylana clung to her father. "Come on, baby," she coaxed, noting the pucker in the tiny lip before she began to cry.

"She can tell you're upset," Holly pointed out.

"Stay out of this!" Candy shouted. "The whole mess of you." Reaching as if she would take the girl by force, she bared her teeth, ready for a struggle.

"I'd rather you didn't," Gary informed her calmly, turning so that Joy was out of reach.

"Fine! I'll unpack the car." The door slammed again as she left, the snow crunching beneath her angry stomps as she reached the back door. Not wearing her coat, the frigid air swirled around her, her body steaming with the fire of her mood. Flinging the back open, she pulled at the items, freeing them and stacking them on the porch.

"What did you do?" Gary appeared dazed, oblivious to anything that had gone on. Sure, his wife had issues, but something had lit the fuse. "One minute everything is great, and the next she's on a holy tirade aimed at you."

Glancing at each other, neither Holly nor Carol made any attempt at a reply. Shifting his gaze to Lanelle, he doubted she had anything to do with whatever had set his wife off. "I see," he mumbled, not really seeing anything but understanding a great deal. "Go get Daks ready for bed, and then we can talk."

"They aren't staying." Candy had opened the back door and struggled to get her mother's wheelchair inside. Fighting with the clunky device burned off some of her rage, but she held on to enough to keep her resolve. "Carol can go pack and get the hell out of my house."

"What? Why?" Caroline demanded, her hands shooting to her hips in disgust. "WE haven't done anything, Candy!"

"She's upset about our relationship," Holly whispered, avoiding eye contact with any of them. "I told you she wouldn't accept it."

Perplexed, Gerald's mouth puckered. "Wait. You guys?" He pointed between them with a free hand, the other still holding Joylana against his chest.

"Don't act surprised," Candy sneered, adding the stroller to the pile of gear in the middle of the kitchen. "I know you guys have been covering for them." She glared at her mother.

"Not my place to say." Still wearing her coat, Lanelle appeared so calm, sitting in her favorite chair and watching the show.

"Yes, it was!" Candy shouted, instantly regretting raising

her voice at her mother, but she was too far gone to care in that moment.

"We should go," Holly implored, reaching for Carol's hand. "Get your things, and you can stay at my place."

Still in a state of shock, Gary stammered, "Candy, are you firing both of our caregivers…because they are gay?"

"No, I'm not firing them and not because they are gay!" she roared. "What have they exposed my mother and my children to? Secrets. Manipulation? It has nothing to do with their personal lives. They have LIED to us."

"They didn't lie to me," Lanelle contradicted her with a matter-of-fact air.

"You should stay out of this." Candy pointed at her, shaking an angry digit. "You knew, didn't you?"

Her mother grinned. She had watched their love blossom and indeed knew all about the romance Holly and Caroline shared. It happened right under her nose, and Candy would have known as well if she had been paying any kind of attention. "We're not hurt."

"We're not hurt," Candy repeated. "What about Dakota? What has he seen? Does he even understand what any of this means?"

"He hasn't seen anything," Carol denied. "We've been very careful not to involve anyone else in the house in our relationship. Here, we have been totally professional."

"Get out," Candy bit back.

"Gladly," Holly huffed, pushing past her and marching up the stairs to pack her lover's things for her.

"I can't believe you're letting us go," Caroline breathed, frozen in place. "I've lived in this house for two years." It had become her home—one she had trusted to be there for many years to come.

"And now you don't!" Spinning on her heel, Candy

marched to the den to retrieve her son. "Come on, baby. Momma's gonna make your bath tonight."

Leaving his toys, he followed her up the stairs where they would get his bath and put him to bed, Candy hoping the women would be gone by the time they were finished.

"What just happened here?" Gary glanced between the only two women left in the room.

"We've been dismissed." Carol sniffed, offering to take Joy from him so he could deal with the mess Candy had unloaded.

"Right. But you and Holly. That's a real thing?"

Caroline nodded, carrying Joy into Lanelle's room. Placing her on the bed, she removed the layers of warm clothing, tears in her eyes as she moved.

"And you knew?" Gary continued, glaring at his mother-in-law.

"Yes," she wheezed.

"Unbelievable." He ran his hand through his hair, his face twisted with a wash of emotions. Candy had kept her volatile condition from her mother, as she did everyone, but he was beginning to doubt the wisdom in that. *Would they have done things differently if they knew the cause behind her emotional outbursts?* His wife had asked him to keep her secret, but he found himself dangerously close to revealing it to save what was left of their household.

Deciding he couldn't violate that trust, he cursed under his breath. Pulling off his coat, he scowled at her. "And you didn't think Candy would want to know?"

"She has eyes." Lanelle didn't waiver. "Not my place to tell her."

"We tried to tell her," Holly cut in. Entering the room, she held a small suitcase packed for Carol. "I tried to explain to her months ago, but she didn't want to hear it. We should have left then, but I wasn't ready for us to be public. Put your coat back on," she instructed, glancing at the slender blonde. "We'll come back for the rest of your things tomorrow."

Tears in her eyes, Carol handed the baby to her father and moved to obey. Her movements slow, she forced her arms into the sleeves, then donned the warm gloves. "I'm sorry," she mumbled, cutting Gary a doleful glance. "I know you are disappointed in me."

His jaw tight, Gary only shook his head, disappointed in all of them. Shifting his gaze to Holly, his anger boiled below the surface, but he understood why his wife was upset. "Just go. You can get your belongings after the holiday." *Some Christmas this is going to be.*

Not arguing, Caroline simply nodded and headed out the door with Holly close behind.

As soon as they were gone, Gary glanced between his mother-in-law and his daughter, as if deciding what to do. He could see in an instant their lives had just become a lot more complicated. Anger roiled in his gut, the uncertainty of their future raging inside him.

"Let me get her put to bed, and I'll come and help you into yours," he offered.

"I can make it," Lanelle assured, struggling to get to her feet.

"Oh, God. No. Let's do you first then." Sitting Joylana down, she stood for a moment, then plunked onto her bottom, her soggy diaper making a *thawmp* sound when she landed. "She needs a change." He knew how; he just hadn't done very many. He winced, realizing their perfectly blended family had dissolved into chaos in a matter of minutes.

Shuffling through the door and into her room, Lanelle made it to the foot of her bed, where she sat again. Following her in, Gary opened a few drawers and located pajamas for her. Her eyes wide, she stared up at him.

"Don't." He shook his head side to side. "Just think of me as your nurse for the night. A male nurse could happen, right? Besides, it's not like you don't have anything I haven't seen before."

Her face sullen, Lanelle realized this, but she would have to face him again in the morning. At the thought of it, she would almost rather sleep in her clothes. "Behind me."

"You want to face away from me. Good plan," he agreed, getting her to her feet, they removed her coat. Turning her around, he helped her undress while doing his best not to look at…anything. Putting the shirt portion on followed by the legs, they got her covered in the warm flannel. "See. That wasn't so bad."

"Thank you." She shuffled around to the side of the bed, where he helped her climb beneath the sheets. Stretched out, she breathed heavily, her exhaustion evident.

If Gary had any doubts about her need for a caregiver, they were removed in a few minutes and a change of clothes. *Damn it.* They had lost a great deal that night, and he had every right to be livid about it. "Goodnight, Mimi," he offered, cutting off the light and dodging out of the room in search of his daughter.

To his relief, she had simply wandered down the hall and had occupied herself with the toys Dakota had left out when he was taken for his bath. "Let's put these away, shall we?"

Joylana grinned at him. "Dadada."

"That's right, princess. Dadada." He smiled, relief painting his features as he sat and let her have a few minutes more. Calmed by the distraction she provided, he began tossing the trucks, cars, and blocks into the basket, with Joy removing a few of them as he did so. "Nice." He snickered. "I'm sorry, but we really need to get you into bed."

Finishing the cleaning, he scooped her into his arms and carried her up the stairs, where he could hear Candy and Dakota still in his attached bathroom they shared with the nursery. Turning left into the nursery, he switched on the heater in her bedroom and closed the doors to keep the air trapped. Starting the water, he sighed. "Something else I don't do very often."

Placing her on the changing table, he stripped her down, poking her belly and earning giggles as he worked the pants off her legs. Removing the diaper, he wrapped her and carried her into the smaller space. Kneeling, he tested the water before he sat her down in the tub. "There you go."

Reaching for the toy bucket, she knew the routine. Helping her to dump it, he didn't dare deny her, despite the lateness of the hour. He needed her to go to sleep, and making her upset would probably not aid him in that cause.

"Everything ok?" Candy's voice cut through his muddled thoughts.

"No, it isn't."

She inhaled a ragged breath. "I'm sorry."

"You should be."

"Are you angry...at me?"

He snapped. "Who else am I going to be angry at?" Grabbing the towel, he lifted Joy out of the tub and wrapped her in the fuzzy comfort. "Excuse me," he spat, pushing past his wife and into the nursery. There, he tended to the drying, diapering, and dressing. Then he snatched up her passy and plunked into the rocking chair.

Once Joy was nestled into the crook of his arm, her small mouth tugging at the fake nipple, he sighed. "Why the hell would you fire them?"

"I didn't exactly fire them. I told them to leave."

"Fired. And what, because they're gay?"

"That's not why, Gary," she denied for the second time that night.

"Then explain it to me," he growled, cutting his eyes up at her. "Because from here, it looks like you're judging them for being lesbians." The word sounded odd, especially when one of the women had once claimed to be pregnant with his child. "If anyone should be upset here, it should be me."

"Yeah, maybe we both should be," she quipped.

"Not funny, Candy."

"I'm not trying to be. All this time, they have been carrying on right under our noses. You know we only hired Holly on Caroline's recommendation."

"I know."

"And apparently my mother knew, and she never said a word."

"I know. But I can't help thinking you wouldn't be this upset if Holly had been a male nurse."

"A male nurse? Why would we have hired a male nurse to care for my mother!" Her voice louder by the end than it had been, Joy jumped.

"Keep it down," Gary hissed. "You can be angry. Just do it quietly."

"Yeah, like that's easy to do," she whined back. "Look. What kind of person do you think I am? I'm not judging them for their lifestyle. It's not any different than people being judgmental about the ebony color of our daughter's skin. It doesn't matter what's on the outside. It's the person inside that counts."

"And you aren't upset because they're two women?"

"No! Even if one of them were a man, I would still be pissed!"

"Because they didn't tell you."

"Exactly!"

"Well, I've got some bad news for you, kitten. Maybe they were afraid to." Letting that sink in, he lifted Joylana to his shoulder. Rubbing her back, he rocked her gently.

"Why would they be afraid?" Candy's voice had deflated, and she hardly whispered the question as if the answer terrified her.

"Look, kitten. I know you've been through so much in your life. I know you are dealing with things in your time and in your way. Not everyone realizes that."

"Don't make excuses for me, Gary."

"I'm not. I'm just saying that I get it. Maybe they don't. Even after two years, have you told Carol all the details? About your mom? About Dakota?" He knew she hadn't told them about her meds. She had a lot of secrets and realistically couldn't expect them to understand.

Candy swallowed, a tear spilling over to streak her cheek. She wiped at it angrily, her eyes burning as she sniffed.

"I didn't think so."

"It's not that easy, Gary."

Every time she said his name, his gut twisted. She spat the word angrily as if he were the source of her pain. "I'm not going to say anything else. I could, but I won't."

"Like what?" She stood straighter, not about to ignore such a loaded statement. "What could you say?"

"You always have it your way. That's what I could say. Because I always give in to you. When was the last time we had a fight? Never? Because I always do what makes you happy. I think keeping your condition a secret from everyone might have been a mistake. I'm sorry I allowed you to choose that path."

"Carol."

"Carol? What about her?"

"We had a fight when you brought her here. And I didn't get my way."

"Name another," he challenged, getting to his feet. Placing Joylana in her crib, he covered her with a light blanket, then ran his large hand the length of her body a few times, stroking her gently. Turning to face his wife after a sufficient pause, he demanded, "Well?"

"I can't." Her face pale, she had scoured her brain, searching for another example, finding nothing.

"Baby, I love you so much. I really do, but I know how broken you are."

"Stop it. I'm not broken." Her mind flashed to the day Holly had called her the same thing.

Stepping towards her, he dared to touch her, starting at the arms. His fingers tenderly exploring her tense muscles, he worked his way up to the shoulders, growing bolder as his palms ran the length of her back, pulling her against him.

Closing her eyes, she sobbed loudly. Her lungs resisting her efforts to breathe, she leaned against him, her hot tears flowing freely.

"Shh," he soothed, his hands working her expertly. "Come on." He nudged her towards the door and into their bedroom, where they wouldn't wake their daughter.

"How am I still stuck in this place?" Her voice cracked, and she slid her arms around his chest, clinging to him as if she might be torn away in her agony.

"Some wounds take longer to heal. It's different for everyone. But you are not alone on this journey."

"I've made such a mess of things," she countered. "The girls hate me. I can't believe they lied to me. And my mother. She covered for them."

"I'm not sure she covered for them, exactly. That would imply she did things to help hide their relationship."

"Well, she didn't tell me. And Dakota? What did he see? His understanding of things is so limited. What if he was damaged by this somehow?" She pulled away from him, wiping at her cheeks as she worried about her son.

"I doubt he was damaged. I'm sure if he saw anything, it wasn't any different than you and I—two people in love, wanting to be close to each other."

Candy swallowed. "I need to sleep. I need to get some rest before I go crazy thinking about all of this."

Stepping back, he nodded. "Sure, kitten. I'll go clean up the bathroom, and you can get into bed."

Lifting her chin, she watched his back disappear into the connecting room. He pulled the plug, and the water slurped at the drain. Her eyes red from crying, she inhaled deeply, then located her sleepwear. Changed and calmer, she curled up beneath the blankets on her side of the bed and hugged her pillow as she waited to fall asleep.

ELEVEN

Sweet Home

BRIGHT LIGHT CUT through a crack in the curtains above the bed, laying a strip of gold across the comforter. Her eyes squinted against the glare, Holly watched Caroline's chest rise and fall in rhythm beneath the blanket. Her golden locks askew, she marveled at her beauty and breathless feeling touching her produced.

Things had been chaotic the night before. Their emotions had run high after Candy had so dramatically thrown them out of her house. *Or tossed Carol out.* Holly didn't actually live there. Pulling a hand free, she traced the length of an exposed arm with the tips of her fingers. *So soft.*

They had never slept together. Sure, they had been building towards it. First touching, holding hands. Stolen kisses. She smiled at the thought of them, the way her heart had raced the first time their lips had touched. *But not like this, naked and unabashed.*

It was the last thing she had expected when they were driving after leaving the Ford residence. Caroline cried the whole way, deeply upset at losing the family she had come to love as her own. But Holly had remained firm, reminding her why it was better that they get out now.

Parking in front of her duplex, it occurred to her that Carol had never been there. Closing her eyes to the morning light, Holly sank into the memory, enjoying the luxurious feel of every moment.

"Come on, love. I've got your bag." They had parked on the street, the neighborhood dark and quiet, resting beneath a fresh blanket of snow.

"Thank you." Caroline sniffed, reaching for the other girl's hand as she led her up the short walk. Arriving on the stoop, she looked around. "It's not at all what I imagined."

"No, it's just a small efficiency. I've been saving, thinking at some point I would buy a house of my own." Flicking the lights on, she looked around at the cramped space, wishing it were more impressive. "At least it's clean," she pointed out with an anxious chuckle, then closed the door behind them.

Caroline took in the room as well. The kitchen, if you could call it that, sat on the right-hand wall, the bathroom hidden on the other side. A closet ran the length of the back. A small table with two chairs occupied the space beneath the front window, and a full-sized bed took up most of the floor space. "Cozy."

"Yeah." Holly giggled, suddenly nervous at having her there. Self-doubt swimming in her thoughts, she placed the suitcase on the table and opened it. "I brought your pajamas and clothes for a few days."

"I won't be needing those."

Holly turned slowly to face her, her mouth gaping. "What?"

Closing the distance between them, Carol exhaled loudly, then reached for her. Only slightly taller, she took command, her hands firm as she ran them up Holly's trembling body. "I've waited so long for this."

As if she were fourteen, reading her best friend's words, her heart raced. "You dumped me," she whispered. "You said you would always love me, and then you dumped me."

"My parents didn't give me a choice." She removed her coat, dropping it to the floor. "No one can stop me now."

Holly shuddered. "What do you mean?"

"I'm going to have you." Carol didn't hesitate, unbuttoning her lover's coat and dropping it as well. Her fingers lithe and quick, she undressed them both while stealing kisses. Her breath in eager pants, she had Holly on edge by the time they had pulled back the blankets and lain upon her soft, cotton sheets.

Kneading her arm more forcefully, Holly toyed with Caroline in the morning light. When she stirred, she pushed herself up and over, straddling her.

"What are you doing?" Still groggy, the night before a haze, she stared up at her.

Giggling, Holly dropped her mouth to the supple neck beneath her, kissing it and dragging her lips across it.

"Don't stop," Carol groaned.

"Oh, I have no intention of stopping," Holly whispered back. "I'm going to drive the memory of every man who ever touched you from your mind."

Pushing against her, Caroline forced her up so that they sat, Holly on her lap, their bare chests facing and tantalizing one another. Pulling at her eagerly, she had no words to express how deeply she loved this woman with her, and as far as driving her previous lovers out of her heart and mind, she already had.

"You ok, precious?" Looped around behind, Carol lay in the crook of Holly's arm. They had spent the entire day making love, only pausing long enough to eat green beans out of a can, not even bothering to warm them.

"Oh, yeah," Caroline moaned, stretching, then hugging her tighter beneath the blanket. Around them, firelight flickered, as they had pulled out and lit every candle Holly owned. "I don't want this to end."

"It isn't going to end. I've got you here, and I'm never letting you go."

Coughing a laugh, Carol pushed herself up to sit, drawing the blanket in around her nakedness. "We ate the only food you had. We'll have to go out sometime."

Joining her, Holly's face flushed. "I never eat at home..." she began, cutting herself off before she mentioned the Ford residence. "Shit."

"I know." Carol sighed. "I can't believe we both lost our jobs on the same day."

"Please don't," Holly begged. "I want to be happy lying here with you. I don't want to think about how other people are going to react. Not yet."

"I don't care how they react. It's twenty-nineteen. Nobody cares if you're gay. Everyone is over it."

"Not everyone. Remember?"

"I remember." Carol grimaced. "But that was a long time ago."

"Not so long." A tear escaped and trickled down Holly's cheek. "My parents never forgave me. What do you think they will say when I present you?"

"I thought you hadn't spoken to them in years," Caroline accused, pulling for more cover. "Are you thinking of making up with them?"

"I guess not." Holly shrugged. "It was just a thought."

"Well, stop thinking that way. Anyone who doesn't like *us* doesn't deserve to be part of our lives." A frown etched on her forehead, her mood was lost. "I have no intention of making up with my family. I've got..."

Holly stared at her. "You've got what?"

"I don't have anything," Carol confessed quietly. "I had a family that I loved. Dakota and Joylana. They were my children. Lanelle. She was my mother." Tears streaked her face. "How could she throw me out so easily? Didn't I mean anything to them?" A low wail built from within until it filled the room.

"Oh, honey," Holly soothed, pulling her in and stroking her wild hair. "It's ok, baby. We've got each other. I know how you feel. I will miss them just the same as you do. I swear it."

"Can we go and talk to her? Tell her how sorry we are?"

"How sorry we are that we fell in love?" Holly scoffed.

"That shouldn't matter," Carol bit back through clenched teeth. "We were professional with our jobs and still can be. I can move here with you..." Her voice trailed away, realizing it would be harder for her to perform her duties if she didn't live there. "Shit."

"We could make it work," Holly quickly agreed, reading her thoughts. "I drive over early every day anyway. Maybe Candy will have to step up a little in the evenings. That's all."

"You make it sound like you want them to take us back." Carol sniffed, clinging to the hope the thought gave her.

"I guess I do. I wouldn't be disappointed. But I'm not going to beg, either." Her fist clenched, Holly shook it. "This is so messed up, and I'm not going to let her walk all over me because of it."

"Oh, baby." Caroline wrapped her in her arms, squeezing her. "You're right. We need to be first. Whatever happens, we are going to hold on to each other." They couldn't be separated. Not again.

"Right."

"So let's get some sleep, and we'll go over in the morning and plead our case. See if we can get our jobs back."

"Right." Glancing at the clock, Holly sighed. "It's almost one a.m. We spent our first twenty-four hours as an official couple making love." Her spirits lifted at the idea of it. "I love you so much, baby."

Wiping her tears, Carol nodded vigorously. "I love you, too. I told you no one would ever love you as much as I did. As I do." Leaning forward, she cupped the girl's face between her hands, holding her in place as she kissed her. Her grip relaxed, she stroked the soft flesh with the sides of her thumbs. "I can't believe how much. So much it almost hurts."

Her fingers caressing the backs of Carol's hands, Holly nodded. "We won't ever be apart. Never ever again," she decreed.

Pushing her back against the pillows, her breathing grew shallow. "One more time," Carol begged. "Then we can sleep."

"Uh-huh," Holly moaned, certain sleep wasn't going to happen in that bed any time soon.

TWELVE

Laying Blame

THE NEXT MORNING, Gary went in to the station, business as usual. As badly as he wanted to stay home with his family, he couldn't bring himself to be Candy's crutch. Not this time. She had made this mess with her self-righteous condemnation, but she would only learn the lesson if she lived the pain.

Of course, things only went downhill from there. Tom had called to inform him that he wasn't coming in for his shift. His son, only a few weeks old, had taken a bad chest cold, and they were at the emergency room.

"Do they think it's serious?" Gary asked with genuine concern in his voice.

"We don't know yet. But they're making us wait and see. We'll know in a few hours if they're going to admit him or send him home."

"Well, it happens." Gary had warned him that he had no idea what he was in for. Regretting his doing so now, he pictured the hospital where he and Candy had spent so many hours after the fire that almost took her family—their family. "Keep me posted. For now, don't worry about the station. I'll cover tonight, and you can take the day shift in the morning.

We'll bump one of the single guys up to cover Christmas Eve night, and Christmas Day is already taken care of since we both get the day off."

"Sounds like a plan," Tom agreed in relief.

"I'll see you in the morning." Hanging up the phone, Gary stared at it for a moment. *Candy isn't going to like this.* Immediately snatching up the device, he didn't care what Candy did or didn't like. This was his life, or a huge part of it. She had told him to come back to it, after all, so she had no complaints when he had to take on his duties full force. "Hey, kitten."

"What's the matter?" He never called unless it was important. It was one of their agreements. No news was good news.

"Tom's baby is sick. I won't be home until the next shift ends."

Her lip quivering, Candy wondered if it were true. "You're not just saying that so you don't have to come home, are you?"

"Don't have to come home?"

"You were pretty upset that I fired the girls," she lamented. "I'm sorry, Gary. I'm so, so sorry."

"Aww, precious," he moaned, her sorrow coming over the line loud and clear. "It's just a shift and bad timing. Don't worry. I'll be home in the morning. Is everything going ok?"

"No, it isn't," she whined, at her breaking point. "But don't worry about us. Be safe, and I'll see you in the morning." The call ended abruptly.

"She hung up." Dazed, he stared at the handset, considering calling her back. Deciding against it, he rested the device into the cradle and leaned back in his chair. "Wow."

A bell shrieked out in the garage. "Damn. That settles that." Leaping to his feet, he grabbed his coat off the hook and bolted through the door. "We got a live one! Everybody suit up, and let's roll!"

He wouldn't have time to worry about Candy or his family that night, as it was only the first call of half a dozen that would roll in over the next few hours. Rushing from one blaze to the next, Gary did what Gary did best; he saved people, saved pets, and put out fires, just as he was always meant to do.

Tom arrived the next morning to find Gerald Ford slumped over his desk, snoring loud enough to rattle the rafters. Chuckling to himself, he stood for a full minute, considering not waking him. Lifting the log from its hook, he ran his finger down, counting the runs. "Jesus."

"Hmm, what?" Gary jolted awake.

"Good morning!" Tom hung up the clipboard and chortled. "Just had to outdo me, didn't you?"

"Outdo you?" Gary stretched, then yawned noisily.

"Seven runs in twelve hours—not bad. Now go home and sleep in your bed. You're leaving drool on the desk."

"Am not," Gary denied, swiping his hand over the flat surface anyway. Grinning, he got to his feet. "How's the kid?"

"Better. Got him on some breathing thing so many times a day. I don't really know. My old lady's handling it. At least they let him go home."

"Yeah. Glad it worked out. Or is working out. I'll get some sleep for sure and be back Thursday morning for my next shift unless you call me in before then." Shuffling towards the door, he felt spent, as if he had been working for days on end.

"You do that, but I'll figure something out if anything else comes up. You need some time off by the looks of it," Tom countered. "Thanks for covering for me."

"Any time." Gary sauntered out through the front doors and around to his Suburban, not looking back.

Candy awoke on Christmas Eve with dark circles under her eyes. Monday had been a fog, going through the motions of caring for her family and things Carol and Holly normally did. Taking her meds, she wondered if they were really helping or if they had put her into the spiral she now seemed caught in.

Gary had gone to work, leaving her alone to face the music. And what a bitter melody it turned out to be. Dakota had a full-on meltdown, Lanelle had fallen in the tub, and even Joy had been cranky, leading to concern she might be coming down with something.

When Gary called to say he wasn't coming home, Candy had sat and cried for ten full minutes before getting up and returning to work. What else could she do? Her family needed her, or at least they did now that their help was gone.

The idea that she didn't measure up kept her awake late into the night, long after she had finally gotten everyone fed, cleaned, and put to bed. Listening to the quiet of the house, she had cried herself to sleep, still wondering how she was going to fix things.

"Wow. You look terrible!" Gary blurted as soon as he came through the door.

"Same to you," she bit in retort, not really joking.

"We had seven calls last night," he confessed, pulling off his jacket. "I was asleep at the desk when Tom got there this morning."

"How's his baby?" She still doubted his alibi.

"They sent him home, so he's ok, I guess." He scrunched

his nose, observing her slouched form. "Did you stay up all night?"

"No. I slept a little." The coffeepot flicked over, signaling the brew was ready. Hoisting the carafe, she poured a mug, then a second. Adding the cream and sugar, she carried them over to the table to sit, waiting for him to join her.

"Is everyone still in bed?" He rolled his eyes around cautiously, noticing the silence.

"So far, yes." She took a noisy sip. "I'm going over to Holly's and begging them to take their jobs back."

"You're going to do what?" His voice dripped with surprise as he pulled back a chair and sat. "Just like that?"

"I can't do this," she confessed, shaking her head. "And not only because I suck at it. I was wrong." She drew a ragged breath. "True, they were awesome caregivers, but in the end, I've lost something far more precious. I've lost two of my best friends. I have to convince them that I'm sorry and hope they will forgive me. I'm not an easy person to live with…or work for. Holly did try to tell me, and I made fun of her. I'm sure it hurt her feelings and that's why they never said anything else."

"Ok." He stared at her, running his fingers around his mouth and smoothing his stubble. Picking up the cup, he swallowed a few swigs of the warm brew. "Thanks."

"For the coffee?"

"For that and for taking care of our house. Our family."

"Pfft," she spat, almost choking on it. "I sucked at it. Mom fell in the shower. It wasn't bad, but it could have been. I knew right then I was in trouble. Then Dakota wanted to go outside, but I didn't want him out there alone, so he pitched a huge fit about that."

"Oof." Gary was much better at talking their son down than she was. "You had a rough day."

"No kidding. I just hope Joy is only teething and not actually getting sick." A tear spilled over, and she swiped it away. "I'm pretty useless, Gary. I have no idea why you put up with me."

"Aww, kitten." He set the cup down and reached for her, pulling her into his arms. "I didn't pick you for your utility."

She coughed a short laugh into his chest. "I'm a tool."

"Stop it!" He burst a loud chuckle himself. "I love you so much, baby. We all have things we are good at. Not everyone is domesticated. What kind of world would it be if we were all good at the same things?"

"I guess not a very good one," she confessed. Nuzzling herself firmly against his muscled chest, she sighed. "I'm glad you're home."

"Me too."

The back door swung open, startling them both. Sitting up, Candy gasped loudly as Carol and Holly both bolted inside, closing the portal behind them.

"May we come in?" Carol asked meekly, shaking her hands as she removed her gloves.

"Without a doubt!" Candy squealed, leaping to her feet to hug her.

"Hey, hey! Easy there," Holly chided, glancing in to peek at Lanelle. Seeing her eyes in the dim light, she grinned. "You ok, Mimi?"

"Better," the older woman croaked.

"Good. We'll get you up in a minute if that's ok."

She nodded, pulling her blanket up under her chin to wait.

"Couldn't stay away?" Gary mused, his mouth twisted into a crooked grin.

Unbuttoning her coat, Holly turned to face them. Candy and Carol were still hugging each other, and she knew they were going to make amends. "Before you get all excited, we need to renegotiate our contracts."

"Oh?" He stood to refill his cup. "What are your demands?"

Releasing her friend, Candy wiped her face with the back of her hand. "Wait. Before you say anything, there's something I need to tell you."

"Always have to be first," Caroline muttered, grinning at the floor. "Ok, madam chairman, let's hear it."

Rocking her jaw, Candice glared at her, only slightly amused by the comment. "I'm a real pain in the ass, ok? I know that. Holly had me dead to rights when she said I needed fixing, but I don't need you pointing that out." Her tone harsh, she could see the surprise wash across their faces, as if she had taken a bucket of cold water and thrown it at them. "Sit down," she commanded, turning to the counter to locate more cups.

Jackets off, the two women took seats, their hands clasped loosely as they laid them on the table.

Eyeing the connection as she served them, Candy grinned. "So, you two really are a thing."

Carol flushed, and Holly grinned. "We are definitely a thing."

"Ok." Candy beamed, happiness exploding within her. "I won't pry as to how serious. But if you have a wedding, I want in."

"Hey, we're not really there yet," Holly corrected, the pink hue of her skin deepening.

"That's ok. I just want you to know how sincere I am." Taking the third seat so their little triangle was formed, Candy sighed.

"I think I hear the baby," Gary lied, making for the stairs.

Alone, the three girls stared at one another for a full

minute. Sufficiently calm, Candy inhaled deeply, then stated firmly, "You have to take your jobs back."

"Wow, that was easy. And here I thought we would need to beg," Caroline teased.

"No begging," her employer quipped. "I'd even offer a raise, but Gary is in charge of the funds, so we'll take that up with him. But I'm certain you deserve one after the day I had yesterday."

"That bad, huh?" Holly quietly sympathized.

"Yeah." Candy shrugged. "I also really need you to know that I am working on me. Carol, you deserve more than I have given you. I should have told you about my past…and Dakota. And even Mom. I'm not tolerating the birth control well, and I'm even on happy pills, not that they work all that great. I really should have let you in. There hasn't been a lot of trust on my part, and I think if I had shared those things, none of this would have happened."

"Oh, Candy. You don't owe me anything. I don't want to hear any of it, really. Not unless you are really sure you want to share. It's not important to me. I should have been a better friend to you. I knew it was dark. It had to be to have hurt you so deeply." Carol blinked rapidly, giving Holly's hand a squeeze. "We all let people down from time to time, but it doesn't mean we don't care."

"Hey, you guys don't get to take all of the blame." Holly grinned at them, their tears somehow comforting. "I want to be angry. I've spent my whole life keeping people away, staying neutral."

"I thought you were nurturing," Candy countered. "Hospice nurses take care of the dying and their families."

"Yes, we do, but not like this." Glancing around, she inhaled deeply, then pushed the air out in a loud sigh.

Reaching with her free hand, she covered her smaller

palm, grasping it firmly. "This became my home, Candy. I let my guard down here in this house."

She cut her eyes over at Carol. "I discovered something I thought I had lost a long time ago. And I realized that caring for your mother is more than a job. You mentioned a raise, and I will definitely take it, but I would care for Lanelle for free if I had to. Just please don't shut me out." Her voice cracked, and her own drops of sorrow glistened in her eyes before they spilled over, dampening her cheeks.

"Good. Does that mean I can get up now?"

The three girls burst into laughter at the older woman's call from the other room. "It sure does," Holly hollered back, giving their hands a squeeze before releasing them. Getting to her feet, she made her way around the table, ready to resume her duties.

THIRTEEN

Forgiving Hearts

GETTING LANELLE UP, Holly felt elated to be back on the job—the one that didn't feel like work at all. "Steady." She pulled the shirt up, helping her get it over her head. "Oh my God. What the hell is that?"

"I fell." It was all Lanelle could say, tears welling in her bright blue orbs.

Her lips pursed, Holly knew throwing a fit wouldn't help anyone, but still. "I'm sorry," she muttered. Sorry she hadn't been there. Sorry Candy had let it happen. Her nose and cheeks grew red.

"It wasn't Candy's fault."

"Did I say that out loud?" Holly hissed, afraid she had.

"No, but I see it in your eyes."

"I'm sorry. I'm just angry that you were hurt." Gathering her clothes, the nurse helped her to dress. "If the blame belongs to anyone, I'll take it. I should have been here."

In the kitchen, Carol pulled out eggs and bacon, getting breakfast started while Candy was upstairs tending to Daks. Her thoughts swirling, she knew there would need to be some forgiving hearts in that house for a while, if not always. She had begun cracking the eggs when her boss suddenly came stomping down the stairs. "What's wrong?" she called, catching a glimpse of her as she rounded the corner and headed down the hall.

"I forgot something," Candy called back, arriving at the office and closing the door with a slam.

"What now?" Gary seconded, joining them with a freshly pampered Joylana in his arms.

"No idea." Caroline shrugged. "She said she forgot something."

The office door opened, and Candice re-emerged, her eyes bright. "I did. I forgot someone I have hurt very deeply these last few weeks."

"Oh, someone else?" Her husband chuckled, not a bit surprised. "Do we need to guess?"

"Your mother, silly. Only, Patrick says they aren't at the condo," she explained.

"Patrick, my mother's butler in Florida? If they aren't at the resort, where are they?" It seemed a little early in the day for shopping, especially on Christmas Eve.

"He said they left for the airport only a few minutes ago. They will be landing back here in a few hours."

"Oh my God. You mean my mother is coming home? I guess she stood it as long as she could." For the second year in a row, Eveline and Roger Ford were cutting their holiday short.

"Longer than she should have." Candy sighed. "I've made a real mess of things."

"Don't worry. I'll find out what time they are landing and be there to pick them up." He grinned at her, pleased she was taking the news so well.

"Bring them here," she insisted. "I need to talk to her, and in person is even better. Then you can take them home."

Family for Christmas

THE SUN HUNG low in the sky as Gary guided his Suburban over the icy streets. He had gotten a small nap, but the long day before wore on his features.

"You look tired, son," Roger observed, sitting in the passenger seat next to him. Glancing at his wife, seated behind him on the driver's side, she appeared preoccupied as she stared out the window. "Relax. I'm sure everything is fine."

"I don't know. I've just had a bad feeling since before we left," Eve moaned.

"Everything's fine, or at least it will be once we get you there," Gary informed her. His eyes crinkling as he grinned, he added, "It's been an eventful holiday this year."

"It has! Is Lanelle ok?"

His gaze flicking to the rear-view mirror, Gary could see her concerned reflection. "I guess so. Why wouldn't she be?"

"Nothing." His mother shook her head. "I just felt…odd. Like something was going to happen to her."

"Is that it? You're worried about Candy's mother?"

"Yes." Her features stoic, she awaited the news.

"She's fine. Really. Everyone is, more or less. We had a bit of a to-do among the girls, but that's all worked out. I guess." Thinking of the girls, he considered if he should drop some kind of hint before they got there. "Carol and Holly have become involved."

"Involved. Involved in what?" Eveline had never liked the girl and couldn't understand why her son had hired her in the first place.

"With each other." The short explanation fell flat, filling the small space.

"Oh my," Roger muttered under his breath, taking to his own window.

"Caroline," Eve spat.

"Yes."

"The girl who lied to us."

"Yes."

"The girl who claimed to be pregnant with your child."

"Yes, Mother. Caroline." Gary shrugged, almost amused at her disbelief. "Caroline and Holly have become a couple. It created a bit of a tiff for the last few days, but it's all fine now," he explained in short.

"A tiff. Candy didn't approve of their relationship?" Roger asked, surprised that she would have such a short-sighted attitude.

"It wasn't their involvement, exactly, Dad. They were hiding it, and Candy took it poorly. But it's all worked out. Everything is going to be fine," he assured, glancing again at the woman in the back seat and hoping it would be true.

Choosing the driveway rather than the garage, Gary parked closer to the porch so they had less snow-coated ground to cover.

Exiting slowly, Eve looked up at the old house. She had been there hundreds of times, but she had never felt such reluctance to go inside. Carefully navigating the slick path, she made it to the steps. One Two. Three. At the top, she paused, her pulse thumping in her throat. Clutching her purse, she held it firmly, as if it were the reins to her emotions as she used it to hold them in check.

Stepping forward, she followed Gary inside, not sure what she would find when she got there. To her surprise, the kitchen was empty, but it didn't stay that way for long. "What's going on?" she demanded as Candy alone joined them.

"We need to talk," Candice informed her quietly.

"Dad, let's see what everyone else is up to." Gary raised a hand, indicating the exit, then following Roger into the other room.

Her lips twitching, Eveline held her bag. "I decided I didn't want to spend Christmas in Florida."

"Ok." Candy opened her palm towards the table, indicating for her mother-in-law to sit.

Removing her coat, Eve took a chair, folding the material across her lap and setting her purse on top. Still holding the leather case tightly, she waited for Candy to take the chair next to her. She had cornered million-dollar deals in her day. What the hell was it about this tiny girl that scared her so badly?

In her chair, Candy folded her hands in front of her. "We make quite a pair, don't we?"

"Who?" Her heart fluttered in her chest, her pulse loud in her ears.

"Us. The two main women in Gary's life."

"Oh. You mean us."

"Yes, us." Candy giggled. "You've been so kind to me, Eve. When I thought you were going to ruin my wedding, you saved it." A tear trickled down her cheek. "Three years ago today, in fact."

"I remember." Her body stiff, Eveline didn't dare look at her. She still couldn't believe Candy hadn't banned that man from further contact when she had the chance.

"It was such an incredible gesture. But even then, I had such a hard time trusting you—trusting anyone, really, besides Gary."

Eve shrugged, blinking rapidly. "I did it for him."

"Maybe. But maybe you did it a little for me and Dakota, too."

The tear escaped, cascading down her aged cheek, streaking her makeup with a dark line. "I'm sure that you were part of it."

Reaching for her, Candy gently squeezed the back of her neck. "Oh, Eve, I'm so sorry I sent you away. I know you only wanted to be here. I know you missed my babies so much while you were away."

Gasping short, spastic breaths, Eve fought for her composure. "Please. We shared the video."

Breaking into loud sobs, Candy couldn't take it. Eve might have will made of iron, but she didn't. She was an emotional mess, and she could damn well cry when she felt like it. "I swear, I'm going to be more sensitive. I won't ever ask you to leave again, and you can come and be part of everything that we do. If you want to. And I swear, I'm not going to complain."

Her shoulders losing their angle, softening, Eve sniffed. "Do you mean that?"

"Yes, I mean that." Candy bawled.

"Then can I see her now?" Her voice shook, and her façade crumbled. Her hand searching, she found a place along the girl's back to apply pressure, hugging her in the awkward position.

Standing, Candy pulled Eve with her. Removing the purse and coat from her grasp, she left them in the chair and led her into the hall and up the stairs. Sitting on the floor of the nursery, Carol and Joylana were stacking blocks and talking to one another.

When her dark eyes caught sight of her grandmother, a wide smile parted her lips, and Joy pushed herself up to her wobbly legs. Making the few steps towards her, she held up her hands and waited to be retrieved.

"Oh, my precious," Eveline breathed. Scooping her up, she cuddled her only granddaughter to her chest, kissing her temple, then pressing her nose against it. "I've missed you so."

Unable to take it, Candy turned, leaving them to the playroom as she lumbered down the stairs. A crackling fire greeted her, the dancing light reflecting off the tinsel of their tree.

"How'd it go?" Holly asked, a bit breathless with anticipation.

"It went well." Candy sat on the edge of the couch, glancing at her father-in-law, who sat next to her. Across the room, her mother occupied her favorite chair, with Gary standing and Holly perched on the ottoman. "Where's Daks?"

"Uh, little man already went to bed. He was terrified that Santa would try to come and skip us because he was awake," Gary informed her smugly.

"Wise boy," Eveline called, reaching the bottom of the stairs, Joy wrapped in her arms. "Will we be welcome for the meal tomorrow?"

"I already said—"

"Yes." Gary cut her off. "Yes. Yes. Yes."

"Good. Then we'll be here," Eve agreed with a grin, bouncing her load a few times. "I have lots of catching up to do."

Candy's gut twisted, she felt the need to openly declare her regrets one last time. "I really am sorry, everyone. I realize that I've been selfish and that all of you have been hurt by it in one way or another." She paused, her eyes traveling the circle of faces. "I was shortsighted and wrong on so many levels. I'm just thankful that my friends and family really do love me and can accept that I'm a work in progress."

"So when do we get to help?" Holly spoke up.

"Now. When I'm being a major pain, please don't be afraid to speak up. I may get upset, and I may even say some pretty horrible things, but in the end, you know, and I know, that I need to hear them." She fell short of explaining her medications. They would learn about that later, maybe tomorrow. For now, she had said what she needed to say.

"Amen," Lanelle whispered, her heart bursting with pride.

"I don't know," Gary countered, grinning deviously. "We can't predict what's in store, and it could be a bumpy ride."

"No, I don't know what's going to happen, either." Candy nodded playfully. "But that's the beautiful thing about life. Even with all the plans we make and the things we are sure about, we still get surprises—like a house full of family for Christmas."

Epilogue

"WELL, GIRLS, WHAT DO YOU THINK?" Standing in the oversized hallway of the house across from theirs, Gary had just taken Caroline and Holly on a tour of the place.

"It's amazing," Holly breathed. "It's at least twice the size of yours."

"It's been remodeled a few times and had two major additions over the years. Yeah, it's pretty nice," he agreed, shrugging his right shoulder as he chuckled.

"We can't let you do this," Carol interrupted.

"Do what?"

"Buy us a house, Gerald. It isn't right," she sneered, placing her hands on her hips as she faced him.

"Oh, umm." He rubbed his chin, toying with her. "Actually, I can."

"And he did," Ben chimed in, entering through sliding doors that led to the side patio. "Ten bedrooms, six baths, and all yours." He held up the key, offering it to his former secretary. "Congratulations, by the way."

Carol flushed, glancing at Holly. "We haven't officially announced anything."

"June twenty-third," the redhead countered. "I'll make sure you get an invitation."

Grinning, Gary clapped his hands together. "It's a lot of house, but being so close to us, Candy and I just couldn't resist setting our favorite help up in it."

Holly frowned at him. "Don't push it, Gerald. You know I could have stayed in my little efficiency apartment or we could have shared Carol's room. We don't really need this much space."

"Well, that might be true," Gary agreed, formulating his reply, "but we do."

Carol gasped. "You do? Are you adopting another baby?" She smiled, clasping her hands together with glee.

"Uh, no. Actually, after the holiday, the doctor adjusted Candy's meds a few times, still trying to find the right mix. Somehow, during all the changes, her birth control failed." He paused there, waiting for them to riddle it out.

"Oh, God," Holly stammered. She had since learned of Candice's eclampsia and the circumstances with Dakota's birth. "You know, abortion is legal. There's nothing wrong with protecting a mother's health."

"I know, but she doesn't see it that way." He turned up his palms as if to surrender. "And in the end, I guess neither do I. We're going to try to have the baby, which means we're going to need Carol's room sooner rather than later."

"Wow!" Carol bounced onto her toes a few times, happy despite the risks. "You know we are going to take good care of her. She has a live-in or nearly live-in nanny and a full-time nurse on the premises."

"That's true. If anything happens, we'll be there as early as humanly possible." Holly's features softened. "She won't be able to take her meds."

"Nope. Things may get a little dicey around the Ford residence, which is another reason it's better if you two have somewhere to go that isn't…there."

"We'll set up a crash room for Dakota and Lanelle as well in case they need to get away for a night," Carol suggested. "What?" She shrugged, catching Ben's doubtful gaze. "We've got plenty of rooms."

"I know." He exhaled loudly, a little sad that things had worked out as they had. "Don't get me wrong. I'm glad you are happy together. It just leaves me wondering when I'll find my better half."

Thank You

Thank you for reading, and I hope that you have enjoyed the 2018 installment of the Sweet Christmas Series. Look for a new adventure for Gary and Candy at Christmas next year. ~ Sam

Books in this series include:
Christmas Candy (2015)
Christmas Eve (2016)
Christmas Carol (2017)
Christmas Joy (2018)
Christmas Holly (2019)
Christmas Lane (2020)

About the Author

Anyone who knows me could tell you, I am a friendly kind of person, never met a stranger and take up conversations anywhere at any time. I work hard, and my mind never seems to shut down, as I wake up often in the middle of the night with ideas pouring out and demanding to be dealt with. Of course that means much of my books were written in the middle of the night.

I grew up and still live in the great state of Texas where everything is bigger, where we have warm weather and a central location. I love my state, my town, and my family, which includes my four sons, my significant other, and many friends as well.

I have thoroughly enjoyed writing this story and hope you will love reading it just as much. And of course, will be many more adventures to come.

You can follow Samantha Jacobey at:
Website: www.SamJacobey.com
Facebook: https://www.facebook.com/SamJac
Twitter: https://twitter.com/SamJacobey

y

hat
here

obey

Also by SAMANTHA JACOBEY

A New Life Series – an epic adventure, TORI FARRELL's life IS one wild story... escaped from a biker gang and running from drug lords... used by the FBI and hoping to protect her present from her past... IT'S DARK - IT'S BRUTAL, and it's WORTH EVERY MINUTE OF IT!! (Mature read, 18+ for graphic sexual content and violence, including rape)

Summer Spirit Novella Series - no one EVER had a summer romance like this… Charlie visits another plane, parallel to our own, where Summer Angels and Dark Angels battle over the fate of man. A unique twist on an old idea that will keep you guessing; will Charlie and Clarisse ever find their HEA? (New adult)

Teach Me to Prey – in this standalone thriller, JASON TRUITT and his friends have gotten their way for years. Deceit, sex, and foul play aren't normally covered in the curriculum, but they're doing whatever it takes to get under BECKY STEWART's skin. When one of the boys turns up dead, it's a race against time to save the others; a STUNNING STORY that will get your heart racing and leave you breathless by the end… (New Adult)

The Binding (Unexpected Magic #1) - One cursed diary will change two strangers forever...Can Meri and Rider use her mother's old book to figure out why someone is after them? Or will the guilty party succeed, ripping the tome away before killing them and then slithering back into the darkness… (New Adult)

The Wicked Awakened (Unexpected Magic #2) – a Halloween novel; a five-hundred-year-old witch wants to turn SARAH MATTHEWS' body into her new home… A twisted tale involving a coven hell bent on seeing that she succeeds. Who will come out on top in this epic battle of wills? (Mature read, 18+ for graphic sexual content and violence)

The Irrevocable Series - From affluent beginnings, BAILEY DEWITT's life has become a broken mess... after her parents died unexpectedly, she didn't think it could get any worse. But when the arrogance of man catches up and puts the entire world into a dooms-day spiral, there will be only ONE PLACE she can run to - the ONE PLACE she wanted desperately to escape. (New Adult)

The Dragon of Eriden Series - Amicia Spicer led a simple life, until she discovered it had all been a lie... On her deathbed, Arely Spicer confessed to her only daughter that she had been found by, not born to her mother and father. Sad news to be certain, the idea of having a family of flesh and blood waiting to be reunited sent the young, independent woman on the adventure of a lifetime. Little did she know, a dragon's heart beat within her chest and her journey would be more perilous than she could have imagined... (New Adult)

Also from our Lavish family

Love on the Double Duo
By L.A. Remenicky
http://mybook.to/LoveOnTheDoubleDuo

The Monroe brothers fall fast, they fall hard, and they fall forever. But the road to true love isn't always easy.

Loving Jessie's Girl – Book 1: Until AJ Monroe left Indiana after college he had always lived in his identical twin brother's shadow. He had made a life for himself in Denver, Colorado, away from Jessie, away from Indiana. But when AJ feared for his brother's safety, he left everything behind to step back into the shadow he thought he had outgrown. Finding his brother was AJ's only concern...until he met Jessie's girl.

Fiercely independent, Rina Abbot hid her true situation from everyone, including her best friend, Jessie. Out of money and unable to care for her rescue dogs she had no choice but to accept the help of the handsome stranger with a familiar face.

Afraid to trust him, she tried to ignore the feelings he stirred within her as they searched for his missing brother.

But secrets never stay secrets for long.

Finally open about their feelings for each other, Rina's secrets began to wreak havoc on their lives. Would Rina's secrets force AJ to give up his dream of loving Jessie's girl?

Beyond Duty – Book 2: After serving in the Marine Corps, Jessie Monroe has finally found a life beyond war. He's focused on

being an EMT and helping his best friend rescue dogs, until he happens upon a curvy blonde stranded

with a flat tire and no jack.

On the run from her past, Dori Graham is slow to trust any man, and she tries to ignore the spark of

interest she feels for her handsome savior, but a friendship grows between them.

When Dori's past invades her new life, Jessie vows to rescue her. Saving her will take him beyond duty

and into his own personal hell. Calling upon his training as a Marine and the depth of his feelings for

Dori, Jessie will need the mental strength to battle to save her and, ultimately, save himself.

Between the Trees
Kathy Moczerniak
http://mybook.to/betweenthetrees

A beautiful coming of age with a dark side that one teenager must fight to overcome...

Beyond Kathryn Lucas' first memory of her father's tree lay a dysfunctional path of violence, heartbreak, and secrets within a family severely entrenched in the vicious cycle of abuse. A lifetime of fear drives her from her home, and the teenage girl finds refuge with an aunt and uncle determined to protect their niece.

Distressing flashbacks unravel in Kathryn's fragile mind among the turmoil encircling her as she struggles through adolescence and descends into her pain-ridden past. When the summation of her unsettling memories allows the darkness to overtake her, she becomes desperate to unearth the light.

Inspired by a true story, Kathryn must hold on tightly to those who love her, searching for her place in a world threatening to break her as she fights to overcome life's betrayals before she is deprived of her future.

The Hunter Series
Sara J. Bernhardt
http://mybook.to/HuntersTril

Jane Callahan is a reclusive, seventeen-year-old high school student dealing with the death of her beloved brother. Her home in Southern California with her mother is a constant reminder of her loss and pain. In hopes of escaping her past she moves to North Bend Oregon to live with her father, where she meets a beautiful boy named Aidan Summers.

Jane is intrigued by his looks as well as his unusual ways of attempting to get her attention. After months of uncommon conversation and frustration, an uncertain romance brews between Jane and Aidan, but Aidan has a ghastly secret that could destroy everything.

About the Author

Anyone who knows me could tell you, I am a friendly kind of person, never met a stranger and take up conversations anywhere at any time. I work hard, and my mind never seems to shut down, as I wake up often in the middle of the night with ideas pouring out and demanding to be dealt with. Of course that means much of my books were written in the middle of the night.

I grew up and still live in the great state of Texas where everything is bigger, where we have warm weather and a central location. I love my state, my town, and my family, which includes my four sons, my significant other, and many friends as well.

I have thoroughly enjoyed writing this story and hope that you will love reading it just as much. And of course, there will be many more adventures to come.

You can follow Samantha Jacobey at:
Website: www.SamJacobey.com
Facebook: https://www.facebook.com/SamJacobey
Twitter: https://twitter.com/SamJacobey

Also by SAMANTHA JACOBEY

http://www.amazon.com/-/e/B00GEB5LX0

A New Life Series – an epic adventure, TORI FARRELL's life IS one wild story... escaped from a biker gang and running from drug lords... used by the FBI and hoping to protect her present from her past... IT'S DARK - IT'S BRUTAL, and it's WORTH EVERY MINUTE OF IT!! (Mature read, 18+ for graphic sexual content and violence, including rape)

Summer Spirit Novella Series - no one EVER had a summer romance like this... Charlie visits another plane, parallel to our own, where Summer Angels and Dark Angels battle over the fate of man. A unique twist on an old idea that will keep you guessing; will Charlie and Clarisse ever find their HEA? (New adult)

Teach Me to Prey – in this standalone thriller, JASON TRUITT and his friends have gotten their way for years. Deceit, sex, and foul play aren't normally covered in the curriculum, but they're doing whatever it takes to get under BECKY STEWART's skin. When one of the boys turns up dead, it's a race against time to save the others; a STUNNING STORY that will get your heart racing and leave you breathless by the end... (New Adult)

The Binding (Unexpected Magic #1) - One cursed diary will change two strangers forever...Can Meri and Rider use her mother's old book to figure out why someone is after them? Or will the guilty party succeed, ripping the tome away before killing them and then slithering back into the darkness... (New Adult)

The Wicked Awakened (Unexpected Magic #2) – a Halloween novel; a five-hundred-year-old witch wants to turn SARAH MATTHEWS' body into her new home... A twisted tale involving a coven hell bent on seeing that she succeeds. Who will come out on top in this epic battle of wills? (Mature read, 18+ for graphic sexual content and violence)

The Irrevocable Series - From affluent beginnings, BAILEY DEWITT's life has become a broken mess... after her parents died unexpectedly, she didn't think it could get any worse. But when the arrogance of man catches up and puts the entire world into a dooms-day spiral, there will be only ONE PLACE she can run to - the ONE PLACE she wanted desperately to escape. (New Adult)

The Dragon of Eriden Series - Amicia Spicer led a simple life, until she discovered it had all been a lie... On her deathbed, Arely Spicer confessed to her only daughter that she had been found by, not born to her mother and father. Sad news to be certain, the idea of having a family of flesh and blood waiting to be reunited sent the young, independent woman on the adventure of a lifetime. Little did she know, a dragon's heart beat within her chest and her journey would be more perilous than she could have imagined... (New Adult)

Love on the Double Duo
By L.A. Remenicky
http://mybook.to/LoveOnTheDoubleDuo

The Monroe brothers fall fast, they fall hard, and they fall forever. But the road to true love isn't always easy.

Loving Jessie's Girl – Book 1: Until AJ Monroe left Indiana after college he had always lived in his identical twin brother's shadow. He had made a life for himself in Denver, Colorado, away from Jessie, away from Indiana. But when AJ feared for his brother's safety, he left everything behind to step back into the shadow he thought he had outgrown. Finding his brother was AJ's only concern...until he met Jessie's girl.

Fiercely independent, Rina Abbot hid her true situation from everyone, including her best friend, Jessie. Out of money and unable to care for her rescue dogs she had no choice but to accept the help of the handsome stranger with a familiar face.

Afraid to trust him, she tried to ignore the feelings he stirred within her as they searched for his missing brother.

But secrets never stay secrets for long.

Finally open about their feelings for each other, Rina's secrets began to wreak havoc on their lives. Would Rina's secrets force AJ to give up his dream of loving Jessie's girl?

Beyond Duty – Book 2: After serving in the Marine Corps, Jessie Monroe has finally found a life beyond war. He's focused on

being an EMT and helping his best friend rescue dogs, until he happens upon a curvy blonde stranded

with a flat tire and no jack.

On the run from her past, Dori Graham is slow to trust any man, and she tries to ignore the spark of

interest she feels for her handsome savior, but a friendship grows between them.

When Dori's past invades her new life, Jessie vows to rescue her. Saving her will take him beyond duty

and into his own personal hell. Calling upon his training as a Marine and the depth of his feelings for

Dori, Jessie will need the mental strength to battle to save her and, ultimately, save himself.

Between the Trees

Kathy Moczerniak

http://mybook.to/betweenthetrees

A beautiful coming of age with a dark side that one teenager must fight to overcome…

Beyond Kathryn Lucas' first memory of her father's tree lay a dysfunctional path of violence, heartbreak, and secrets within a family severely entrenched in the vicious cycle of abuse. A lifetime of fear drives her from her home, and the teenage girl finds refuge with an aunt and uncle determined to protect their niece.

Distressing flashbacks unravel in Kathryn's fragile mind among the turmoil encircling her as she struggles through adolescence and descends into her pain-ridden past. When the summation of her unsettling memories allows the darkness to overtake her, she becomes desperate to unearth the light.

Inspired by a true story, Kathryn must hold on tightly to those who love her, searching for her place in a world threatening to break her as she fights to overcome life's betrayals before she is deprived of her future.

The Hunter Series
Sara J. Bernhardt
http://mybook.to/HuntersTril

Jane Callahan is a reclusive, seventeen-year-old high school student dealing with the death of her beloved brother. Her home in Southern California with her mother is a constant reminder of her loss and pain. In hopes of escaping her past she moves to North Bend Oregon to live with her father, where she meets a beautiful boy named Aidan Summers.

Jane is intrigued by his looks as well as his unusual ways of attempting to get her attention. After months of uncommon conversation and frustration, an uncertain romance brews between Jane and Aidan, but Aidan has a ghastly secret that could destroy everything.